GERRY JONES

THE
SIN EATER

BARRIE & JENKINS
LONDON

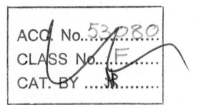
© Gerry Jones, 1971
First published by Barrie &
Jenkins, London, 1971
Printed in Great Britain by
Butler & Tanner Ltd,
Frome and London
ISBN 0 214 65279 3

Set in 11 pt Linotype
Baskerville

FOR MY WIFE AND CHILDREN
DOROTHY, GARY AND REBECCA

In Welsh custom there was, in each neighbourhood, a man who for a few shillings was called to take upon himself the sins of the newly dead.

He spread salt on the breast of the dead person and with the salt a piece of bread. This he then ate, thereby devouring the sins of the deceased. He was detested and treated as an outcast. This man was called the sin eater.

ONE

David James, alone in the train compartment, huddles into the corner and presses the side of his face against the hot glass. Twenty-five years old with dark Welsh good looks, a strange mixture of confidence and insecurity, a combination he knows will never leave him.

Eyes stare unblinking as the English countryside speeds past in a burned blurr this summer day in 1914. Hedges, grass, soil, fences, smoke . . . images clicking on the unblinking eyes, and dying there. The mind somewhere else . . . with his Mam, thin, hugged by a pinny, moving cold about her tasks, building walls with silence. . . . With brother Iorweth, head growing from the valley formed by his high pointed shoulders, smiling his secret smile. . . . With sister Jenny, young, sweet Jenny, walking with him in the teasing wind, no need for words . . . pieces in a jigsaw . . . Jenny's head on her shoulder, hair a waterfall down her arm.

"One day," she says, her voice suddenly strange, "When we're both grown up . . ." She stops. David comes close.

"Well?"

Jenny leaves the thought to float, gets to her feet and runs swiftly down the slope to the river. She never answered, not then, not ever. David would die still wondering.

The train passes from England into Wales, cutting

7

its way through Shrewsbury, hooting its whistle and sending a seagull vertical with fright. David stirs, the images in his mind break. His eyes focus on the passing landscape. Wales settles about him, a hot blanket that covers the sleeping face and brings with it dreams of drowning.

In a distant field a domino dog chases itself in the heat. Farmhouses, suspicious of the sunshine, stay huddled at the feet of mountains and sheep stand limp like summer snowflakes.

Snow. The kaleidoscope regroups, another picture forms. Snow. Winter. January smashing the familiar into an icing cake. A snowman with a carrot nose and a scarf hanging sad with wetness. David and his Dad running black scarecrows against the white backcloth, hooting with glee, stumbling, churning the surface, making patterns with their happiness. Holding hands in a curtain of snow, doing a daft and giggling dance, idiots close to nature. Mr James falls on his back, his mouth open to swallow air and snowflakes melt on his teeth.

"The best snowman in Wales, boy," he yells. "We've made the best snowman in Wales."

Pieces in a jigsaw.

A scream of metal, the contact of hot glass on his forehead and David's eyes focus. On a rise in the ground a couple picnic with Sunday sandwiches. A ribbon of river appears to be moving, climbs upwards and hides behind a belt of trees. Horses stand desolate, twitching. Cottages . . . a man sitting on a stone bridge . . . a village wobbling in the haze.

The letter. If only the landlady had told him the letter had arrived. Not that it would have made much difference except for the business with Helen. Helen was nineteen, a year younger than David, but being brought up in London instead of a Welsh farmhouse she was in many ways in advance of him.

When David had first arrived in London, paddling cautiously in the new society, suffering the laughter at his accent, he had met Helen and become attracted. He often invited her to his lodgings and they'd talk

8

of fashion, or the theatre, which Helen liked, and sometimes they'd go to the river at Richmond. He knew that the time would come when he would make love to her, it was a bridge to be crossed.

Helen, though, instinctively refused to crack the foundation on which his life had been built. Refused, that is, until last night in the darkness of his bedroom. And then the letter which he hadn't noticed.

The train snorts its way upwards, feeling its age on the incline. The landscape falls away and David looks down on a tiny village. A wind is beginning to whip the sides of the train and bend the trees. Dark, storm-filled clouds wait on the sky's horizon for the sun to finish its fun. David closes the carriage window, sees a bird buffeted high then swoop in an arc down the side of the mountain and level out over a church tower where the clock has lost one of its hands.

The clock. . . . David closes his eyes. The grateful train begins its descent to the valley. The storm clouds start their gentle charge. The clock. Ticking. In the bedroom, Helen slowly and theatrically removes her satin dress. David watches her, lust, like too much food, heavy in the pit of his stomach. She lies back on the bed, wearing only her knickers and her stockings and she smiles and begins to writhe as though already making love.

"Come on, David." He pulls off his jacket, unties his tie, kicks off his shoes and then just stands there, lost in hell. Real hell too, full of ogres and brimstone and the eternal flaming pit of the damned. A hundred remembered sermons boiling in his blood.

"Come on," says Helen. "Come on, love, it'll be all right, really." She scrambles from the bed and tears at the buttons of his flies.

"Come on, come on." Her mouth goes close and David moans the devil from his mind. His fingers slide into her hair, his nails scratching at her scalp. Suddenly they're on the bed, Helen gasping, and his hand travelling up the stockinged leg, past the knee to the stocking

9

top. The bed is creaking and groaning with them . . . the flesh at the top of the thigh, so white, so soft, so warm.

Helen, shouting now, like someone being burned. His fingers move to the knickers, press under the elastic, like soldiers creeping under barbed wire. He feels the mound of hair and moans and they twist and jerk out of control. His trousers fall away from him sliding from the eiderdown and breaking their legs on the floor.

A beam from the street light escapes the curtained window and, like God's birchrod, smacks his bottom. Deep inside his mouth Helen's tongue is probing and licking and cracking his skull and his eyes starting to close in that little drowning see the letter on the table by the door and with a shock that dries his lust he recognises the writing.

Scrambling from the bed to the table he tears open the letter. Helen lies rigid on the bed, a prisoner waiting for an execution squad that suddenly didn't fire. He hurriedly reads the short letter and a stillness settles over the room. Helen turns on her stomach.

"What the hell are you doing reading a *letter*? What the hell are you *doing*?" For a moment he doesn't move, just stands there without his trousers, the letter glued to his hand. Then he turns to her as though surprised to find someone in his room and even more surprisingly on his bed.

"It's from my Dad, about my sister Jenny . . . she's dead." A lifetime then of silence. A drunk sings outside. Helen moves slowly to the corner of the room, picks up her dress. A minute later she is gone.

In the train carriage David changes his position, raising his feet on to the seat opposite. He notices a dusty patch on the far window, stares at it, then comes beside it. His forefinger traces a pattern in the dust. The lines go in and out, cross and re-cross, double back on themselves, squares in squares in squares. He destroys it with his coat cuff, returns to his position by the other window, places his head against the glass and becomes involved in a race with a rain cloud.

North-west down the track the village station of Llandeth, which earlier had soaked the sun and lost its edges, now cools itself in the gathering wind. The posters which had hung by their feet like thin carcasses, begin a gentle flap. In the station approach Daniel Davies, having stretched his legs for the second time, pats his horse and climbs back into the trap. He sits in stillness, only the thumb moving, stroking the reins.

The shadow from the station gable lengthens slowly, covers the dusty yards, until the grey tip of it breaks like a wave over the horse's hooves. Elwyn Price, the station master, walking deep in flowers, stops, places his pipe in his mouth and looks across the station approach at Daniel with his horse and trap. They wait like statues, solitary, unmoving, figures in a Welsh Western.

Daniel is a small monkey of a man, fifty last birthday and desperately eager to reach his three score years and ten. This particular span has become almost an obsession with him, no one in his family yet attaining it, although his father had gone close, reaching sixty-eight and dying on the lavatory.

Daniel's face is a walnut, both in colour and appearance and contrasts sharply with his white hair. A Plynlimmon type, from the black mountain district, small and dark. Once his hair had shone like raven feathers. The body is squat and over-rigid, the forearm muscles fat worms above the soil-grimed hands. The legs are lost in corduroy but the years haven't taken away the bounce. A tough little man, then, sculpted by wind, rain and hard work, but keeping in his eyes as much kindness as you could ask for.

From his waistcoat pocket he takes his prized fob watch and clicks open the silver lid. He sees that it's still two hours before David arrives, returns the watch to his pocket and turns up his collar. Being excessively early for appointments has always been both his vice and virtue. The story used to be that Daniel arrived before his parents married, but now they say he arrived before they *met*.

Unusual with Welsh countrymen, this concern with time, preferring as they do to calculate in seasons, treat clocks with suspicion and keep them only for company. To Daniel, though, if punctuality is the politeness of princes, being too early can only be an improvement and to hell with them. He lowers his head to his chest, glad in some ways not to have to face David just yet. As the wind tinkles the horse brasses, he slips into sleep.

When David arrives, just under two hours later, he walks from the station entrance and finds Daniel still with his head on his chest, snoring gently. Elwyn Price, watching from the gloom of his office cell, lights his pipe and smiles. The evening has come in black and angry, the wind whipping at angles. David shakes Daniel's arm. The tired eyes open.

"David," cries Daniel. "Master David, here let me take your bag." He scrambles from the trap, stiff with sleep. "My word, my word, how you've grown. How you've grown, boy."

TWO

The horse and trap pull away from the station, the
wooden wheels clattering the cobbles and wobbling out
of true. Daniel stares ahead, he speaks without turning
his head.

"Comfortable?"

"I'm all right, thanks, Daniel."

"I . . . I'm sorry about . . ." He stops.

"Thank you, Daniel."

Daniel pauses, letting the wheels clatter in the silence
between them.

"It's difficult to talk," he says after a while.

"Yes . . . it doesn't matter."

Daniel still stares ahead, narrowing his eyes and peer-
ing with great intensity down the road, as though navi-
gating the horse and trap is a matter of great complexity
and skill. Difficult, though, to imagine anything easier,
the road being deserted and the horse capable of finding
its own way to the farm, blindfold.

On they go, down Station Way, over the stone bridge,
past a clump of thatched cottages, standing like little
loaves, and begin the slow rise to Nant-Glyn Pass. The
Welsh Sunday hangs in the air like starch. Trees drip
piety, roads glisten with respectability. Dogs half-daft
with boredom bark at the passing wheels then gasp out
their hopelessness and return to the smell of polish and
seed cake. Daniel turns his head.

"Going to have a storm, I reckon. If this wind drops

13

it'll bucket down." The words are torn from his lips and thrown away. David leans forward.

"What?"

But Daniel doesn't hear. They travel for a mile in silence. Over the hill Monday morning, sick of Sunday, waits. But first the fervour, generated since the earliest waking eye this morning, must find release. Daniel points his finger.

"Look, Master David," he says, "Saint David's Chapel." Cuddling the foot of a hill, small, unfriendly, leaning against the wind, packed inside with hot humanity. It is here, inside the stone walls, underneath the wooden roof, among the sickening smell of candle wax and sight of ageing flesh and bird bright eyes, that the fervour is released.

The Reverend Williams, his biblical head shedding sweat like juice from a squeezed orange, pauses, and burns his glare into the congregation. He's been going at it now for twenty minutes, blistering the worshippers, beating them, lifting them up and now he stops and asks for a glass of water. It is passed up to him in a reverential silence and he drinks quickly and deep. There'll be another fifty minutes or so yet, they'll get their money's worth tonight, they'll get it all right.

He casts aside the glass and seems about to spit into a bucket like a wrestler ready for the next round. The 'Hwyl' is on him now. Christ on the cross dies in his eyes and the congregation shout their delight at the lash of his tongue. For fifty more minutes the Reverend Williams, his feet in the centuries of tradition, roars his sound, pounds his fists, claws at the air, stabs with his finger, pleads, implores, begs, orders, weeps, and finally collapses in a thunderous silence of approval at his performance. For a while he remains motionless, as though death has come upon him in his moment of exaltation, then he slowly turns and leaves the pulpit.

Once again he's worked the spell to last a week, used

14

his 'hwyl' like a circus strongman flexing his muscles, and if God in the quiet of Heaven isn't clapping then, in the humble opinion of the Reverend Williams, he damn well ought to be.

Outside the chapel, David passes by, listening to the hymns in the wind putting a seal on his homecoming. Daniel, uncomfortable with the silence, breaks it.

"This old place must seem pretty bleak after London, Master David."

"Bleaker than anywhere," says David. The silence comes back for a while. The horse clops on, unaware of tension, eager only for his nose-bag, his head down, his hooves hammering the road. Daniel, like a fighter not knowing when to quit, wades back into the conversation.

"I'm sorry about Jenny . . . she was a lovely girl."

"Yes . . . well . . ."

Their thoughts are tied by string to a post.

"The times I've seen her, Master David, running through the fields, laughing so happy. Poor little Jenny . . . I sometimes wonder what God's playing at."

And David, his head down low, wonders what God is playing at too, as the trap moves on into the distance. It grows smaller and smaller until from the chapel, where the worshippers now emerge with their sin washed for a week, the trap looks like a small cube of black sugar. It disappears into the dusk, where ghosts and Welsh goblins watch and shiver.

Five miles away the James' farmhouse, set alone in the vastness of the countryside, waits for their arrival. Inside Mr and Mrs James move like flotsam in a whirlpool, not touching. Beyond, in the polished parlour, Iorweth sits by his sister's coffin, the candles making glow-worms of his eyes.

Later, in the dark outside, a horse snorts and a wild dog barks.

"Here we are, Master David," says Daniel, leaping nimbly from the trap and offering his arm. "Home safe and sound."

THREE

Daniel flicks the reins and without looking back clops off into the night, leaving David standing sick with sorrow. In his blood he feels a long, sad whine of misery like a one-note fiddle. Ahead of him the farmhouse waits, mangled dry of welcome.

It's a farmhouse like many others in this fastness of Wales, strongly built of stone, capped by a slate roof, it lies low, pushing itself into the landscape. At the back is a large orchard and immediately to the left a wooden barn. This contains some of the farm implements and bales of hay stacked to the ceiling, giving off the special smell that is as much a part of David's childhood memory as the long early walk to school.

His legs, divorced from his mind, move forward. Flesh and blood in independent motion. The soul of him watches his body cross the yard, enter the shadow of the doorway, sees his arm, devoid of wish, open the door. Sees him enter the house, close the door, sealing out the wind. Watches him walk down the narrow hallway then pause for a minute by the grandfather clock before turning the brightly polished brass knob of the living-room door and entering.

The room is as it always was, everything exactly in its place, untouched, unmoved, permanent, a museum. At the mean windows heavy brown curtains, given a cheerless gaiety by dark green piping, hold deep shadows in

16

their folds. The focal point of the room, a fixed black grate, with a boiler on one side and an oven on the other, is attended by two chairs, one a rocker, which permanently face and watch, like cats comfortable in its glow.

On the wall above the grate a gun hangs and beside it horsebrasses flicker brass stares in the light of the two oil lamps. In the pool of darkness by the door a sad mahogany piano bares its unplayed yellow teeth. There's a deep scratch on the piano top, made by David when he was seven years old. Although his mother, who at this moment is sitting in the rocking chair ignoring his entrance, has rubbed years of polish into the wound, the scar remains, sometimes covered by a photograph of dead people on a picnic.

By the door the Welsh dresser, shining with thickly applied varnish, holds its three rows of best plates, a model of respectability. Two tables, one large and covered with a purple cloth, the other small, spiral-legged and smugly supporting a heavy leather-bound edition of the Bible. Plain, uncomfortable dining chairs sit back against the wall, wallflowers at a dance.

Mr James, soberly suited, rises. Black hair thinning, compensated for slightly by a luxuriant moustache. Once handsome, now running to fat, an adventurer trapped in an alien environment. A good farmer, of course, dedicated, hard-working, he survived the agricultural depression and now operates a much smaller farm, concentrating almost entirely on livestock. Yet, though he appears every inch a countryman, as his forefathers have been down the generations, there's a restive spirit at the core of him that denies the relief of acceptance. He moves forward, his arms outstretched.

"David . . . it's David . . . good to see you, boy . . . good to see you." The arms wrap David in a bear hug. "Oh, David, boy." David, uncomfortable in the male embrace, is glad the suitcase in his right hand gives him an excuse not to respond.

"Hello, Dad." His voice is low and has no warmth.

Ignoring the coolness of the meeting, Mr James continues to hug his son as though determined to find a spark.

"Dewch," he says. "You're frozen, boy, come on . . . come on and get warm, now." Lowering the suitcase, David crosses to the grate. For a second he stands in the glow then turns his head in the direction of the rocking chair.

"Hello, Mam," he says, the words cautious, probing. Mrs James is staring down at her hands, resting on her lap. A silence. No answer. David turns to look at his father, who, hating the atmosphere, tries a smile which dies at birth.

A thin woman, Mrs James, wrapped tightly in black, a closed umbrella. She had been beautiful once, the photographs proved it, but now her manner was stick stiff and the black, high-collared dress, relieved only by the panel of lace on the breast, uses her body as a coat-hanger. The beauty and grace, which in yesteryear had caused young men to become almost obsessive of their appearance and heartbroken at her marriage, had long ago evaporated. Only in the unexpected brightness of her eyes and the thickness of her old grey-black hair is there a reminder. She speaks, without the slightest trace of movement.

"It's been a long time."

"Yes, Mam, a long time."

"You haven't changed much." Surprising, this remark, as she hasn't appeared to look at him since he entered the room, gazing only at her limp and folded hands.

She rises from the rocking chair with a strange, undisciplined sense of deportment, as though hoisted upright by a string attached to her head.

"Are you hungry?"

"No, Mam."

A pause. The clock in the hall makes itself heard. Mr James, who has been standing on the edge of the atmosphere like someone waiting for a balloon to pop, moves forward.

"Come on now, boy," he says, putting an arm round David's neck, his voice over-hearty with nerves. "You must be hungry . . . I mean . . . a long journey like that." David looks into his father's eyes, recognises the quiet desperation there, nods and smiles,

"All right, I'll have something . . . but not much, I'm not hungry, honest."

Mrs James moves like a poker to the small back kitchen and David sits in his father's chair, stretching out his legs. Flicking imaginary dust from his lapel, Mr James moves to the rocking chair, sits, and gazes at his son, smiling foolish fond. From the back kitchen comes a clatter of pots.

"Not much of a welcome from Mam," says David.

"Well . . ."

"She still hates me, doesn't she?"

"No, it's just her . . ."

"It's all right, Dad."

Mr James sails in on another tack.

"Well, well, you're filling out nicely. London seems to suit you." He leans forward, tapping David on the knee with his forefinger. "I'll tell you something, boy, I wish I'd gone to London when I was your age . . . wish I had." Tap, tap, tap, on the knee. "Wish I had." He smiles into David's face, a sincere smile too, no messing.

"I'm sorry the reason for my coming home is such a sad one," says David.

"Well . . . well . . ." The smile fading, the light going out of it.

"It doesn't seem real."

"Tell me, boy," says Mr James. "What's it like in London?"

"When I got your letter . . . about Jenny . . . I didn't know what to do. I just walked about . . . just walked."

"No . . . well, there it is." The smile has gone.

In the kitchen there's another rattle of crockery.

"Don't you want to talk about it?"

19

"Not much."

"How's Iorweth?"

"Still the same, still the same." He sits back in the rocking chair and for a while it is a creaking substitute for conversation.

"Where is he?"

"In the front room with Jenny." He takes in David's puzzled look and goes on. "He sits in there with her hour after hour."

David rises slowly with the air of someone going nowhere in particular. He gazes down at the grate, runs his finger along the black-leaded top and eases towards the piano, stretches out his hand as though to touch the piano's awful mouth but lets the hand drop, the note unstruck. Suddenly he moves to the door.

"I'll go and see him."

Mr James, past caring now, rocking in his private misery says, "All right, but careful what you say now."

"Don't worry, I know him."

Mr James gets up quickly from the rocking chair, which, free of its burden, bobs madly in relief, crosses the room and grasps David's hands like a sick one thanking a faith-healer.

"Honest to God, David," he says. "It's good to have you here."

FOUR

From the oil-lit kitchen David moves into the candle-lit parlour and in every flickering corner there are a thousand ghosts of childhood. Unloved, these Welsh parlours, kept only for the unlaughing times, formal meetings with best cups. Spirits of gentlemen with polished boots talking boringly forever as dust drops silently through a sunbeam. Brittle ladies in bombazine, some talking with a half whisper, some watching with a half smile. David closes the door and walks in among the memories.

In the centre of the parlour four plain chairs support a coffin. The four candles stand guard at the corners. Iorweth, wearing dark trousers clamped at the waist by a broad leather belt, and a collarless striped shirt, sits with his back to the door, staring without motion at the coffin and its occupant.

Eighteen years of age is Iorweth, pale and painfully thin. His eyes have a mystic, opaque quality as though life were going on in his head and the eyes simply showed the shadow of it. His hair is long and reddish, hiding the ears and curling in the nape of the neck. Impossible to tell if he is aware that anyone has come in, so still and trance-like is he sitting. Then he speaks.

"Come back then? We've been waiting."

"Hello, Iorweth."

"Come to visit your sister? Looks like she's sleeping doesn't she? Peaceful."

At the word 'peaceful' the breath from his mouth flickers a candle flame, then it steadies itself and comes to attention. David moves forward, reaches out his hand and touches Iorweth on the shoulder. Beneath the hand the shoulder eases away from contact.

"Don't touch me, David. You know I don't like you touching me."

A silence. Wasn't there a clock once? . . . In the corner? . . . A china clock with people dancing? Iorweth lowers his head nearer to the coffin, his eyes staring, unblinking.

"Yes, looks like she's sleeping. It broke her heart when you left, you know."

"She understood," David replies, but in his heart he knows he's lying. "Aren't you going to look at me?"

Iorweth slowly turns his head, tilts it and stares at David, much the same as he's been looking at Jenny.

"You haven't changed," he says.

"That's what Mam said."

"And Dad?"

"Dad was pleased to see me."

"Like always."

"Like always."

Iorweth rises, smiling a little. There is a chest of drawers in the corner, been there always, got roots in the floorboards. Iorweth crosses to it and rubs his hand on the shining top.

"You shouldn't have come back, you know," he says, .as his hand planes the surface. "You've no place here."

"This is my home."

Iorweth laughs, a sudden bark of a laugh and in this parlour and at this time, it's an obscenity.

"People who pack their bags don't have homes." His hand planes the surface wildly and unconsciously.

"Tell me about Jenny," says David. Iorweth's hand stops, a dustbin lid coming to a halt after being knocked over by a night cat.

"Tell what?" he asks.

"Just tell me about her."

22

"You know what happened, I found her hanging in the barn . . . she killed herself . . . you know what happened. We've tried to keep it as quiet as possible—but there's been talk." Iorweth's voice, deliberately flat and factual, is hinting at something beyond the obvious.

"Talk?"

"You can still see the marks on her neck." David's eyes take in the rope burn necklace, then back to Iorweth.

"She'll go to Hell, you know, David."

"What?"

"Everlasting torment." A plain fact, beyond discussion, indisputable.

"What are you talking about?" asks David, walking innocently into Iorweth's trap.

"Didn't Dad tell you? In the letter?"

"I know nothing."

"They don't want to talk about it, I suppose." Iorweth's words are bringing the walls in closer. David goes after the bait, bites on the worm.

"What happened?"

"She was pregnant."

David feels the hook go in. "Oh God," he says, and Iorweth begins the slow reel in.

"The wages of sin is death."

"Is that all you can do? Spout religious cant?" David is fighting, but Iorweth is the fisherman, the moment is his.

"You should never have come back." David comes in close.

"Jenny was the sweetest, most lovable girl and God in His mercy . . ."

Iorweth reels him into the shallows. "No mercy for sinners," he says.

"God in His mercy . . ."

"Shall I tell you why she let the boy make her pregnant?"

David waits, still, helpless. "Why?" he asks.

23

"Because he looked like you," says Iorweth. "She told me so . . . because he looked like you."

David cries out "Iorweth"—it is a cry of pain, a plea to make the truth not so.

Iorweth has landed his fish. He crosses to the window, pulls back the mourning curtains and stares out at the night. The sad sound of rain can be heard, dancing on the outside foliage. Little individual raindrops break free from the mass, hurl themselves against the window, turn for seconds into pearls then, dizzy with the success of their transformation, wobble dazedly down the pane and join the stone sill's conformity of wetness.

On the window ledge David notices the china clock with the dancing figures.

"It's started to rain," says Iorweth. "Black, heavy clouds over Craig Valley. Can you hear it beating on the flowers outside? I suppose it will be raining when we bury her tomorrow."

David moves in close behind Iorweth. "Who did it," he asks. Iorweth draws the curtains, then turns and speaks in a faraway voice.

"Did it?"

"Who's the father?"

The faraway voice goes on. "The rain will churn the fresh dug hole, down will go the wet coffin, they'll spade the liquid soil on her . . ."

"Who's the father?"

"Black umbrellas cracking in the wind—Dad crying —Jenny gone."

"Who's the father?"

"Father of what, David? Father of what?"

A pause and a candle splutters. Iorweth walks to the door, turns.

"I'm going to bed."

The door opens, closes, and David stands alone and spent by the window. A creak in the corner as a floor-board stirs in its sleep. A candle coughs, sighs and sends up its spirit in a spiral of black smoke. David holds his breath . . . breathing will disturb unnameable dreads.

24

The door opens and Mrs James stands there in a triangle of light.

"There's some tea out here waiting for you," she says.

"Thank you."

"Been talking to Iorweth?"

"Yes."

"What did he say?"

David just stares at her, unanswering. Oh God, if only he could run across the room, take her in his arms, kiss her, hug her. If only she'd hug him, hug him, hug away the years. They face each other like duellists.

"He's a good boy," says Mrs James.

"He said Jenny would go to Hell."

"A fine lad."

"Because he never went away?"

"A fine boy," she says.

"You didn't tell me about Jenny . . . about her being pregnant."

They face each other in the ghost-filled room, silence putting its finger on the agony. Say something, Mam, say you're sorry, say you're sorry and I'll stroke your hair and nothing will matter, not ever.

"I'll go and put some more hot water on," she says. "So you can have a second cup."

She goes, leaving the door open.

David opens the curtains, stands where Iorweth stood, looks out. Outside everything is weeping. London is a million miles away, and Helen, and walks in sunshine by the Thames. He picks up the china clock, runs his fingers over the delicate pattern, strokes the dancing figures. They've danced through the years, these china people, danced without moving, right back to childhood. They've mutely watched it all, watched and stayed frozen, smiling forever at something, happy forever because of something. His hand moves to the key at the back. He turns it half a dozen times but there is no tick, the clock is broken. He puts it back on the ledge, pulls the curtains across the night and leaves the room to its sadness.

Mr James is sitting staring at the fire as David enters. "Soon be over, David boy," he says. "Soon be over."

"Don't pretend she never existed, Dad, please don't."

"Then back to London, I suppose?"

"Isn't either of you going to talk about it?"

Mr James leans forwards and stabs the fire with a heat-twisted poker. Gas breaks through the cracks in the coal, catches fire, then fades. Sparks burst and leap for their lives on to the carpet. Mr James leans back. David moves to the door.

"I'm going to bed," he says.

"So soon?"

"I'm tired."

"But you haven't touched your food."

"Which room am I having?"

"Your old room."

"With Iorweth?"

"Yes."

"Tell Mam I've got no appetite."

Mr James is up from the chair now, moving across to David, taking his wrist, talking in a confidential whisper, urgent.

"David, it's not that I don't *want* to talk about little Jenny . . . it's just . . ."

"All right, Dad."

"Things are as they are and there's no point in . . . no point."

"I know," says David, taking his hand away. "Goodnight, Dad."

"Goodnight, boy. God bless." David goes out and Mr James returns to his chair. He stabs at the fire, again and again and again. Smash, smash, crack, the poker splinters the coal, flames run along bridges of gas, crack, crack, the poker thrusting like a piston, breaking, destroying.

"Where's David?"

"He's gone upstairs, said he didn't feel like eating."

Crack, crack, the last reluctant piece of coal bursts open, its belly on fire.

26

"Alice, love, in the name of heaven show the boy a bit of affection, for just once in his life."

Mrs James, teapot in hand, turns and goes out into the back kitchen. She takes off the teapot lid and throws the contents into the sink. Mr James appears in the doorway, the poker still in his hand, glowing angrily.

"Please, love, please."

Mrs James looks at him with dead eyes, picks up a fluffy towel, slowly wipes her hands and says

"It's going to be wet tomorrow."

FIVE

The bedroom hasn't changed. . . . Time, it seems, is
trapped there. From the marble-topped table the oil
lamp throws a circle of yellow light on to the ceiling
and in this fairy ring the whitewash bubbles and flakes
like the surface of the moon. In the corner a spider's
web, whose sticky threads had once made busy flies
motionless, hangs torn and catches only dust. Tired
floral wallpaper hangs from habit on the walls and the
paper roses with their roots in paste can be wiped away
by a finger.

David, still fully clothed, sits on the bed, his head
resting against the brass bedhead, his legs stretched out,
his hands deep in his pockets. From his position he looks
straight at the door where too much brown paint hangs
in curtains down the panels and the white door knob,
cracked into a thousand fine veins, stares sightless like
an eye in a Roman statue. Beside the door, above the
wash jug and soap dish is a painting of an Arab and
camel walking in moonlight. Welsh dampness makes
green-brown explosions in the desert sand.

Lying in bed, Iorweth, his hands clasped behind his
head, his eyes open, stares at the ceiling. On the wall
above him a sixpenny Jesus, memento of a trip to Car-
marthen, hangs by glue from a wooden cross.

For a while David lies unmoving, listening to the sad
sound of rain outside falling through leaves. Then he

brings his knees up and hugs them, resting his chin on the cloth hill.

"You know," he says, "I've often thought about this old room of ours—hasn't changed. Same picture, same smell, same window—waiting for Santa Claus—he never came, did he?"

Iorweth remains staring at the ceiling, silent.

"But then I never believed he would," says David, subtly changing course. "Not like you—you believed hard. You believed in fairies and ghosts." David releases his knees and half turns to face Iorweth.

"I never believed, did I, Iorweth?" he asks. "Did I?"

For a second or two Iorweth doesn't answer, then he says,

"Not even in gentle Jesus, you didn't believe."

"Not even in gentle Jesus."

"Jenny believed in Jesus. She used to cry because He was dead."

David gets off the bed, tugs his tie off and throws it on the washstand.

"Yes, I've often thought about this room," he says, "and do you know what I've thought of most? More than the warmth and tickle of blankets and standing by that window washing in freezing water on a winter's morning before school . . . more than all that, Iorweth. Do you know what I've thought about?"

Iorweth doesn't answer, but his eyes say "What?" David pulls off his waistcoat.

"I've thought about how Mam used to come in and kiss you goodnight . . . just you, not me."

He throws the waistcoat across the back of a chair. A slow smile comes to Iorweth's face, the eyes are more opaque than ever.

"Listen to the rain outside," says Iorweth. "A wet, black night and Jenny in Hell."

"Stop talking like that," says David, undoing the buttons on his shirt.

"Don't you believe in sin, David?"

"I suppose I do, but Jenny was no sinner."

29

"Oh, but she was, she was." His eyes close, for a moment it seems as though he has dropped unexpectedly to sleep then his eyes open and he says casually,

"And Dad's a sinner, too."

David gives a short laugh. "What are you talking about?" he asks, pulling off the shirt, grimed with travel.

"He's a sinner, David." The voice is flat, almost sad. "The father you love is a sinner."

"You're talking rubbish." The crumpled shirt is thrown into an embrace with the waistcoat.

"Am I?" asks Iorweth.

David moves across to Iorweth's bed, pushes his face in close. "Rubbish," he says, his face an inch away.

"Well then, let me tell you something about Dad," says Iorweth.

"It'll be lies."

"Not lies, David, not lies."

David moves quickly from the bed, picks up the water jug, pours some water into a bowl and soaps his hands. He lowers his hands into the bowl, leans on them, stares at them, two white stones in a murky pond. Iorweth has baited the hook again. David bites.

"All right then, what? . . . About Dad . . . what?"

"Some years ago," says Iorweth, and the words seem practised, "Dad and me went fishing, in that little stream, you know, by the Devil's Gorge. Well, it had been a good harvest that year, bumper, and Dad was drinking heavy. He told me about a girl in Cardiff, told me about the things he'd done with her."

David takes his hands from the wash bowl, shakes them and picks up a towel. He dries his hands slowly, a finger at a time, seeming to be over-absorbed in the task. Iorweth goes on.

"This . . . incident in Cardiff was when he'd only been married to Mam for a few years. Jenny was only a baby and you too young to know anything."

David strokes his finger-nails as though alone in the room.

"I remember," says Iorweth, the voice growing

harder, "I remember him sitting by that stream, the bottle in his hand, roaring with laughter and saying that he hoped one day I'd find myself a girl like that. The next morning he took me to one side and said I wasn't to mention to anyone what he'd said—that he'd only been joking. But I could see his eyes, David. He hadn't been joking, and I've never forgot."

David puts the towel back on the hook, crosses to the bed and kicks off his shoes. One under the bed, the other clatters to the corner, lies on its back and shows the hole in its sole.

"I don't believe you."

Iorweth sits up. "You believe in nothing," he says. "You're empty."

David gives another short laugh, but he knows he's losing ground.

Iorweth is out of bed now and the shadow of him is a monster on the ceiling.

"You too have your sins, David, and be sure they'll find you out."

"You're talking like a mad thing."

"Do you know why Dad liked Jenny so much? Because they were two of a kind. That's why he likes you, too."

"And I suppose you, Mr High-and-Mighty, are free from all sin?"

"That's right," replies Iorweth, pleasant now, absorbing David's remarks into cotton wool, making them impotent. "Me and Mam. She's always known it . . . that's why she kissed me goodnight, not you." His voice grows hard again while David plumps the pillows. "You've always wanted Mam's love, haven't you? As long as I can remember. You used to lie in bed crying when Mam kissed me and then went out. You'll always cry, David, always."

David turns. "Shut up," he says, and the words are a crack across the face.

But Iorweth goes on, a waterfall now. "Even if you run to London or right across the world you'll never get Mam. You'll cry till the end."

31

"Mad."

"There's only one road to walk, David, only one road."

"I've done no bad, no bad ever."

"You should never have come back."

"My sister Jenny—*our* sister—is lying down there . . ."

"Never have come back. This is *my* room now."

Suddenly there is silence in the awful bedroom and the childhood ghosts stir like maggots. David moves away, picks up the shoe with the hole and throws it to its partner under the bed.

"Well, I'll be gone soon enough," he says. "Back to where there's light and life and a few smiles."

"I thought you liked this place better," says Iorweth, and he laughs. "I thought you said you liked this place better."

"I do," says David, "but it's spoilt. I've never been able to see that misery is next to Godliness. If indeed it is, if indeed Heaven is full of your sort, Iorweth"—his voice is rising now and Iorweth smiles—"if it is, then I hope that Jenny *has* gone to Hell and I hope I join her. I hope that Jenny and Dad and me will dance through the everlasting fires."

The door opens and Mrs James stands in the black mouth of it. David sees her there, feels his heart turn over, feels the years fall away. He's a child again, wondering, hoping, praying.

"What's going on," asks Mrs James, sheltering in the shadow. "What's happening?"

"Sorry, Mam," says David.

Iorweth has leapt into bed like a three-year-old, pulling the clothes about his head. Mrs James moves from the door and the lamp puts craters in her face.

"We've got to be up early tomorrow," she says, and her eyes taking in David's carelessly discarded clothes make him feel childish, foolish.

"Yes, Mam."

"Right, then," says Mrs James, "no more noise now. Goodnight, Iorweth." She stoops down over the bed, kisses Iorweth lightly on the forehead. "Sleep well." She moves to the door and without turning, goes out.

David, in his vest and pants, stares for long moments at the door and the ghosts stir again. Iorweth pulls the bedclothes from his face and says in the flat and factual voice,

"Just me, you see, David. The kiss—just for me."

David stands submerged in the ghosts, his eyes filled with the brown door weeping paint. And the rain outside a sound that will last forever.

SIX

David's eyes open and the first sound he hears is the rain. He tries to slip back into the anaesthetic of sleep but it's no good. Outside in the yard Dad is talking to Ben, a farm worker. The wild dog barks somewhere beyond the orchard.

This is it then—Jenny's day. He pulls himself reluctantly from the warmth of the blankets and notices for the first time that Iorweth's bed is empty. From the window he looks down on to the farmyard and sees his father, an oilskin over his head, running in a cocoon of rain towards the barn. There's not much to be seen from the window today, the weather has put a wall around the place and anyway the land around, with its endless stone bridges, bent shrubs and ugly mountains growing like boils out of the flat, is so depressing that even rabbits scream with boredom.

Hard to imagine really that it was only yesterday morning he had walked in the heat of the sun in London, and later from the train carriage window had seen the horses twitching away the flies, the couple picnicking by the ribbon of river and the little village wobbling in the earthquake of haze.

He goes slowly down the stairs, listening as he goes to Mam and Iorweth talking in hurried whispers in the back kitchen. He enters the freshly polished parlour, the smell of it making sickness in his stomach. Jenny lies

34

still, in the release he craves. He bends slowly to kiss her forehead, her skin wax apple. Then Mam comes in and says,

"It's time you were dressed."

In the bedroom now he wishes he could go down on his knees and pray, but the bending and the praying won't come. Not now, not ever, it seems. Rakes his teeth over his lips, lips that still hold the wax apple feel of Jenny's skin. Wishes hard he hadn't kissed her, feeling the kiss to be an insult. Too late, though, too late for everything, and he gets into his clothes and hears the downstairs laugh of Iorweth and the downstairs voice of Mam saying "Shhhhhh" and the memory voice of Jenny in his head, and the memory of her tears.

"Jenny, Jenny, why are you crying?"

"I can't sleep, David."

"What's the matter?"

"It's you, going away . . . it's terrible."

"I've got to go."

"Oh, David, love."

Shuts his eyes now to cut out the memory, opens them to look long at the picture of the Arab and his camel walking forever in the same square of desert and the never-ending, unchanging moonlight and the shadows hanging like discarded black stains from the motionless bodies.

So he finishes dressing, looks at himself in the mirror, seeing only shapes, and feeling control has gone from events, he goes downstairs and joins the slow motion hurry of the funeral.

"Arabs, the lot of us," thinks David, "stuck forever. Only Jenny has got out of the picture."

They come for the coffin and soon a white angel, hands chiselled in permanent prayer, face raised to the sky in wet ecstasy, stands like an emissary a few yards from the mourners, catching the rain in her stone eyes.

It's falling thick in moving, close-packed, vertical lines, dashing itself to bits on contact. David, the water beating at his uncovered head and running in rivulets down his face, blows it away in spumes. Ricocheting from the headstones into a seeping mist it clings about him, absorbing itself into the layers of his clothing and chilling the surface of his skin. Beneath his feet the unanchored soil is in constant motion. A saying from his childhood—about rain—"Angels crying". David lowers his head and the rain pounds it, a tap washing a lettuce. The nearby trees with roots feeding on yesterday's people are sick of the constant beating and droop hopeless.

A voice then, in his cold, wet head. Jenny's voice, and a memory of another time, and a look on her face, and tears.

"Jenny, Jenny, why are you crying?"

"I can't sleep, David."

"What's the matter?"

"It's you, going away . . . it's terrible."

"I've got to go."

"Oh, David, love."

"I've got to go, I can't live with the feeling in this house."

"It's going to be sad without you."

"Jenny . . ."

"I'll have no one."

"Dad loves you."

"Yes."

"I'm sorry, love."

"What time are you going?"

"Daniel's picking me up with his cart at about five in the morning . . . I'll be gone when you wake."

"No, no, please wake me, I want to see you off."

"No point, love, better I go when you're sleeping."

"Oh . . . oh . . ."

"Now don't cry . . . it's not for ever, Jenny . . . one day I'll come back, I promise."

A bell clangs, steady like a timeless drum and David feels the rain again.

"David . . . David?" It's his Dad talking.

"Hmm?"

"You all right, boy?"

"Yes."

"Here, throw a handful of earth on the coffin . . . a way of saying goodbye."

It's got to be done . . . tradition . . . so David throws the wet soil and watches it splatter against the coffin lid and slide away to smear the brass handles. It's got to be done . . . tradition . . . but to David, among the waiting trees, with their hungry roots, it seems like the final insult.

SEVEN

David and his Dad sit at home, stone gnomes in a dark garden. David shivers and Mr James is glad of the crutch to conversation.

"Hell of a day for a funeral, boy, hell of a day."

"The first funeral I've seen—horrible."

"Yes, well . . ."

"The rain seemed to get into my bones."

"Yes. Different from when we buried your granddad. July it was, and so hot we could hardly breathe . . . so hot." His voice fades and he stares at the fire as though he can see a picture of the day there. "I remember that when they lowered the coffin into the grave it was covered in wasps . . . covered."

A dog barks outside in the distant wet. David leans forward and the movement is sudden and unexpected, putting Mr James on guard behind his frightened eyes.

"Why is Mam so different from you?" asks David. "You've always talked to me, played with me, we've had some wonderful times . . . but I'm nothing to Mam . . . nothing."

"Well your Mam . . ."

"What's so special about Iorweth, answer me that."

"Now, don't worry yourself," says Mr James, patting David's knee. "Don't worry about it."

"What's so special about him?"

"I can't answer these questions."

"Well, what's wrong with me, then? What's wrong with me?"

"David, for pity's sake . . ."

"For pity's sake why can't I get a kiss or a kind word from my own Mam?"

"*I* love you," says Mr James, walking pointless to the window. "*I* love you."

"And Jenny?"

"I loved her, too."

"And Iorweth?"

"He's different."

"Yes, he's different—and Mam's different."

Mr James stares hard out of the window, sees the sky getting even darker by Craig Point, wishes he was there now, free—anywhere, away from David, questions.

"It's always been like this," he says, the voice unfriendly. "You and me—her and Iorweth. Why bring it all up again?"

"Because Mam's behaviour to me drove me from my own home. Why am I being punished?"

"Punished?"

"Yes. Punished."

"Punished? Punished?" the word bites and David is blinking with the unexpected anger of his Dad's question. "Punished? What do you know of punishment, David? When you've lived as long as I have you'll know of punishment. For God's sake, boy, stop torturing yourself with things that won't change. It's always been like this, always will be . . . always . . . always."

"Always Iorweth the apple of Mam's eye?"

"Always."

"Always you and me like uninvited ghosts?"

"David . . ."

"And different, different Iorweth. Iorweth with different hair and eyes and nose. Different Iorweth. He's not your son, is he? He's not my brother, is he?"

"How dare you say that," shouts Mr James, a worm of a vein on his temple. "How dare . . ."

"It's true, isn't it? True?"

39

"God forgive you."

"True, isn't it?"

"Now that's enough."

"Enough?"

"Enough, enough, enough."

"It isn't even . . ."

"I've never heard . . ."

"I want to come home, Dad, I want to stay."

"There's no more to say."

"No more?"

"No more to say."

"Don't bury me like Jenny, dry-eyed."

"I love you David—don't make me change."

"Dad . . ."

"Don't make me change—you're all I have."

"Dad, I love you, but we can't go on pretending. I can't go on punishing myself. Iorweth isn't one of us, is he?"

"All I have," says Mr James.

"Is he?"

"David . . ."

"Say it. Go on, Dad, in the name of pity—*say* it."

"David," says Mr James, and he comes in closer resting his hands on David's shoulders and putting pleading in his eyes. "David, you've always been my favourite, you know that . . . always you . . . but there are things we can't talk about."

"Never?"

"Things best forgot."

"Never, Dad?"

"Tell me about London. Tell me about your friends there."

But David is moving quickly to the door.

"I'm going for a walk," he says.

"But it's dark, it's late," says Mr James. His words, though, fall on the closed door and he moves around the room, aimless in the prison of himself.

David moves away from the house, suddenly stops as he sees a light shining in the barn. He moves forward, pushes open the vast and creaking door that has been a million meals for worms, and enters. Having come through the curtain of barn smells David pauses, then on a mound of hay he sees Iorweth lying. David comes a bit nearer, drops a question down on Iorweth.

"Why are you in the barn?"

"How did you know I was here?"

"I saw the light of the lamp. What are you doing?"

"Oh, just lying in the hay," says Iorweth, just lying in the hay. "And smelling the drying rain and thinking."

"Thinking about what?"

"Oh, this and that," says Iorweth, "This and that . . . and Jenny . . . this is where she killed herself, you know."

Iorweth stirs and props himself on one elbow. "It was cold at the funeral, wasn't it, David?" he says. "I saw you crying too, David. Or was it just rain? Just rain on your face?"

"I cried all right," says David.

"Big Welsh crocodile tears."

"What do you mean?"

"Who were you crying for? You or Jenny?"

"I don't understand."

"No," says Iorweth sitting up. "But I think *I* do. There's no point in crying, David, for things lost. You can't bring them back."

David turns slowly, like an old man, and crosses back to the barn door.

"I'm going for a walk," he says.

The barn door slams to and David moves quickly, stumblingly away from the farm and begins to run down the lane where the wind is singing as he moves in his private marathon of agony. His mouth is open . . . remembering snowflakes melting on teeth, a snowman, Dad laughing, a thousand years ago, Mam's eyes watching. Runs . . . runs . . . his tie curling from his Adam's apple, feels the trees shake raindrops on him for cool. Cries out now when the stitch grips his side, stares out beyond the early stars.

41

Then the cemetery, pushing open the iron gate to the dead, his feet running on memory through the gravel chippings and drowned flowers, runs, stumbles, as an owl hoots in the lonely patch of black by Jenny's grave. He kneels then and drops his words, heavy and endless sorrys.

And while David kneels there, four miles away in the village Alun Rhys, alone in his bedroom, beats his hands on the wooden arms of the chair until he cries in pain.

Alun looks at his fine, pain-filled hands then rubs them, then crosses to the window and looks out at the night. Nineteen years old, good looks, a sensuous mouth. Nineteen years old and a clerk in an office. The ink marks your heart for life. Paper rustling, nibs scratching, clocks ticking, men sniffing. He looks out at the night. He should have gone to the funeral today, should have gone. In spite of everyone he should have gone, he owed it to Jenny. Jenny . . . a name that would stick with the ink. He turns from the window and sits on the bed and the white-washed walls move in like regimented infantry and the ceiling moves down six inches. He rises, moves to the door and goes out before the bedroom eats him.

Down the staircase, along the bit of brown hall and into the living-room. It's an awful and cluttered room, this, filled to excess with the bric-a-brac of countless long dead lives. In the corners shadows on the walls like blots and at the centre of a shadow a spider in his web, Mr Rhys sits shrunken behind his steel spectacles. Beside him Mrs Rhys reads a book with a composure that almost removes her from her situation. She could be a ghost.

His sister Annie watering flowers at the window table, stops and is surprised to see him come in. Mrs Rhys looks up from her book with that wax composure then snaps the book shut and the snap asks, "Why?"

"I couldn't stay up there any longer, that's all," says Alun. "Is there any tea to drink?" Mrs Rhys stares at him fondly as though looking at the monument of someone once loved who has died. Mr Rhys removes his spectacles, holds them near his mouth and blows a mist of breath over the lenses.

"Don't put too much water on the flowers, Annie," he says. He polishes the glasses with a dazzling white handkerchief, then returns them to the bridge of his nose. Mrs Rhys goes back to the pages of her book and Annie carries the rose-painted jug of water through to the back kitchen.

"I asked if there was any tea," says Alun. "Aren't you going to speak?" No answer. Except that the silence is a terrible answer in itself. He goes through into the back kitchen, takes Annie by the arm and turns her to face him.

"Aren't they ever going to talk to me?" he asks, "Is this going to go on and on, just because of that one thing?"

That one thing . . .

Alun, feeling young and fit, the blood bubbling with happiness in him, half walks, half runs in the cleavage of the valley while above him birds whirl in their own world. He lies on his back under the tree where as a boy the armies of his mind fought themselves to a bloodless death every Sunday, and watches a white cloud change from a mountain into a ship then break slowly and beautifully into bits.

Then, suddenly, in a dress of cornflower blue Jenny is running up the rise towards him, calling his name, waving her hand. He gets up and rushes towards her, falls full length, gets up again and carries on running till their fingers link and they spin around and both fall down like ring-a-roses.

"Look what you made me do," he cries. "You made me fall down and mess up my shirt." He shows her the great grass stain on the front of his shirt.

"Serves you right for being clumsy." She's lying on her back laughing, with her feet in the air.

"And you're too cheeky, Jenny James." He moves

at her suddenly and falls again. Jenny laughs like a maniac then, and Alun charges after her . . . up the rise, past the childhood tree, and in the dip beyond Craig Point he catches her by her cornflower blue sash and pulls her to the ground.

"You're mad," he shouts with the breath he's got left, "mad as a hatter." Then they're both laughing and yelling and wrestling, squeaking and snorting like things gone silly and the birds above just circle silently, making no comment.

After a while they calm down and propping themselves on their elbows they stare with half smiles at each other. Fourth meeting smiles, smiles showing awareness behind the pleasure that they're moving to the invisible point beyond which hurt can happen. Lie there now like love's young dream, but it's really just a sort of daftness, a tickle of the spirit, a careless drift that brings them to kiss and then embrace, then make love, then separate —hot, breathless, showing shock and wonder at what has happened.

For a long time they lie in silence, as though by keeping still they will stop the world's clocks ticking, the hearts beating, time waking up, moving on, making what they have done into history. There is probably a split second between living and dying and there's one between a deed instantly regretted and the stroke that makes it fact. Alun and Jenny lie in the long split second. Then Alun speaks, and there's no going back, only a future of facing things.

"How is David getting on in London?" he asks. He wonders why he's thinking about David.

"All right, I think," answers Jenny, and there's a sudden ache in the heart of her. She has, for a moment, a vivid picture of David in her mind, the flash of detail that sometimes comes when the mind lets go the consciousness and floats free. There is no vivid picture of London, though, it's just a place where David is.

EIGHT

London in 1911, though, is much more than just a place
where David is. It is vital and bustling and alive and
another planet away from Wales. He walks lonely in
the long, unfamiliar streets, aching to be home yet hating
the thought of it. Every inch of him feels strange, every
inch a foreigner.

Shortly after his arrival in London he found lodging
at 3 Belton Road, a terraced house owned by a Mr
and Mrs Albert Shaw, and a spacious room at the top
of this rather ugly house became his home. The house is
like many others in the district, six rooms, a back
kitchen, and a small garden at the back where mainly
sweet peas grow.

David enters by the front door, moves down the short
hall past the living-room which also serves as a kitchen.
The door is open and he sees Mrs Shaw standing among
her Windsor chairs, large scrubbed table, dozens of
saucepans and ten cannisters, drawing off some hot water
from the boiler. It's a cheery room, this, and the light
sparkles on the polished fender, the shiny lino and even
the brass tap from which she is drawing the water.
Cheery, too, is Mrs Shaw, though God knows why, thinks
David.

"Hello, David. All right, love?"

"Yes, thank you, Mrs Shaw."

"Settling down a bit, are you?"

"Yes, thanks."

"Your friend has called to see you . . . whatsisname? . . . Emrys. He's waiting in the parlour, you can talk to him in there if you like." Although David has his own room he knows that Mrs Shaw for some reason would prefer him to entertain his friends in her parlour so he says, "Thanks."

"Supper in half an hour," she says.

David goes down the narrow passage and enters the parlour. Emrys Price is sitting there in a red plush chair. The room is rather cold and feels like a place for storing ornaments. There are too many wooden shelves, a large threadbare carpet with an old stain in the centre of it and an old piano over by the window that has had so much polish rubbed into it it's sick of preening.

"Hello, David," says Emrys and moves towards him offering his hand. Tall and thin is Emrys with a thatch of red hair and piercing pale blue eyes, in his early twenties.

Although born of Welsh parents he has lived all his life in England and yet in spite of this, or perhaps because of it, he is a fervent Welsh Nationalist. The drawers of his desk at home are filled with fevered writings on the history of Wales and its destiny.

This fanatical interest in a land he has only once visited, and that for a short spell, has made him considered to be something of an oddity, and not surprising. His fervour reached a peak last year with the industrial strife in South Wales which led to twenty thousand being made idle at the pits and rioting breaking out in Tonypandy. The officer commanding the Hussars, Sir Nevil Macready, moved in and gave orders for his troops to open fire on the demonstrators. Proof enough to Emrys, this, that the Liberal victory of 1906 and the ministerial appointment of Lloyd George was anything but a victory for the Welsh, it was nothing other than a betrayal.

So, working like a saboteur from the inside, he makes it his business to get to know any expatriate Welsh he can, and in hours of animated conversation further the cause of Home Rule.

He holds small meetings in his uncle's sunhouse and here he and a few disciples let off steam. David knows about these meetings but hasn't, as yet, been asked to attend one. It's as though Emrys is carefully weighing him up, and not being too pleased with what he finds.

"Hello, Emrys," says David, "I didn't expect to see you today."

"Well, as a matter of fact," says Emrys, and his voice, belying his rather Welsh appearance, is very educated English, "I think I can fix you up with a job."

"Oh?"

"Yes, a chap I know, works for a newspaper, thinks he might be able to get you in."

"That's wonderful."

"He's Welsh, too," says Emrys, casually examining his rather dandified appearance in the wall mirror. "Of course it all depends on how you get on . . . what he thinks of you."

"Of course," says David, but his heart sinks, for he knows what Emrys means, and if he's got to be a patriot for the job then there's no point in bothering. Emrys gives a final tweak to his bow tie and turns to face David.

"His name's Bob Roberts, he could do you quite a bit of good."

"Thank you, Emrys, it's very good of you."

"Not at all," says Emrys, picking up the straw boater he had placed on the what-not. "That's what friends are for, isn't it?" A pause, then. They look at each other, there's a bit more yet.

"As a matter of fact, David," Emrys goes on, "he's coming to one of my meetings tomorrow night. It would be a perfect opportunity for you to meet."

"Look, Emrys, I'm not very interested in . . . well, in . . ."

"All you've got to do is come . . . no obligation."

"All right."

47

"Good. You know where the place is, don't you?"
David nods. "Fine. We'll be starting at seven thirty."
"I'll be there."
"Excellent."
Emrys moves, stick stiff, to the door, and turns.
"Oh, I almost forgot," he says, the words measured, modulated, filled with Oxford. "I've acquired myself something of a girl friend. She's very nice and not at all . . . shy . . . if you know what I mean."
David knows what he means all right but he only says:
"Oh? Look, I'll show you out."
"Thanks. She'll be at the meeting tomorrow, you can tell me what you think of her."
"All right."
"I respect your judgement of people, you see, David."
"Thank you."
"Seven thirty then. By the way . . . her name's Helen."

She's lovely, too, sitting there in the sunhouse, the dark colour of her costume showing up the paleness of her face, while the late sun behind her shoulder sets her hair on fire. A face too fine and intelligent to be really beautiful, but enough promise in the eyes to keep a troopship happy. David knows that Helen's eyes are watching him in the shadow of her large, floral straw hat, but he leans back nonchalant in the uncomfortable chair and tries hard to listen to Emrys.

He knows his facts and figures, does Emrys, stabs them home with a finger on a cane table. God, it's boring, though, and hard to think of Lloyd George, or Emrys ap Iwan with his fanatical pamphlets, or the folk heroes of history that Emrys drops like spit from his lips, Gruffydd ap Llywelyn, Hywel ap Maredudd, Owain Gwynedd—on and on with the sun going down and Helen watching. Emrys leans forward on the table, his pampered hair now streaked across his forehead with sweat.

"Eleven years ago," he says, "and . . ." He lowers his gaze to a grubby piece of paper he is holding in his right hand. "I quote . . . Lloyd George said 'While England and Scotland are drunk with blood the brain of Wales remains clear and she advances with steady step on the road to progress and liberty'." He pauses and then goes on: "Since that time the cause of Home Rule has known its moments of elation and despair, but today there is a new vitality within the movement, a new hope, and we, friends, are part, a very important part of that vitality, that hope."

A ripple of applause, then, from the assembled few that sounds like half a dozen babies' bottoms being smacked at birth, but David feels only the ache of boredom and Helen's hypnotic gaze. Emrys, mopping his brow with a spotted handkerchief, hands over to Bob Roberts, the chap who works for the newspaper and might be able to do David a bit of good.

David focuses on this chance for a future and sees only plastered hair, eyebrows that shake hands on the bridge of the beaky nose and uneven, discoloured teeth. Yellow teeth, broken teeth and the words hissing through them and fouling the air. All the ghosts are summoned again, the bones rattled and the foul breath is just launching into a study of the Mabinogion when David suddenly rises and moves to the door. Emrys leaps up and catches him by the arm.

"What's the matter, David?"

"You, that's what's the matter, the whole, bloody lot of you. Now let me go."

A pause . . . God has stopped the clock.

"You're not being very polite, are you?" says Emrys.

"I'm not feeling very polite, I'm bored to bloody death."

Such a lot of bloodys from David, he's surprised really. Surprised too at his own anger, can't think why he's so upset by all this Welshness. Why should he be? What's the reason? He doesn't know, he only knows he is. He wrenches himself free from Emrys' grasp.

"You're bloody stupid, Emrys," he says. "Don't you know that? Pig bloody stupid."

"Get out," screams Bob Roberts from behind the cane table, "Go on, get out!"

"Don't worry, I'm going," says David, "You're like a lot of mediums calling up the dead, that's what."

"Dead!!" yells Emrys. "You're talking about your country, Wales, Cymru, your past, your future, your flesh and bones . . ."

"Go to hell," shouts David, pulling open the sunhouse door and running out into the gathering gloom. Emrys turns round to the shattered group, his eyes piercing the corners for further signs of betrayal. Bob Roberts wipes his yellow teeth on a brown handkerchief.

"Take no notice, Emrys," he says. "We shouldn't have asked him to come. Good riddance."

Emrys sits slowly in one of the chairs, crosses one leg over the other, dangles an arm on the arm rest and gives a little laugh which is meant to sound like a return to his foppish indifference but which comes out like plaster for his plinth.

"Yes," he says, "my fault for asking him, still we live and learn."

Helen comes over, then, and stands above him like another nail in his coffin.

"Yes, we do, don't we," she says.

"And what's that supposed to mean?" asks Emrys, in his chair and studying the toe of his shoe.

"I mean we live and learn. I've learned about *you* tonight. You're weak, aren't you? It's strange I've never noticed it before."

"Don't say any more, Helen, it would be rather foolish of you."

"Very, very weak. I thought you had a sort of passion, but it's only a sort of sickness."

"Thank you very much. Anything else?"

"No, nothing."

Helen goes out, leaving a silence hanging like toothache in the summer-house.

Bob Roberts moves with extended hands towards Emrys and attempts to extract the silence.

"Look, Emrys," he says, smiling yellow. "Take no notice, it's just . . ." But Emrys leaps to his feet and the others, who have been nothing to the evening but claps and nods, shrink in their skins as Emrys kicks violently at the cane table and sends it crashing into the corner.

"Go home," he shouts, "the meeting's over."

David is half a mile away when Helen catches up with him. They talk for a minute or so then begin to walk together, then David laughs, then Helen reaches out her hand and David takes it and they walk like that into the London night where the posters advertise everything.

His eyes focus on the dim outline of Jenny's grave. The night has eased around him, the stone of the grave turned to yellow in the sudden moon. Oh, Jenny, I'm sorry, I'm sorry. I didn't know it mattered so much, my going away. I had to do it, had to find some sort of life.

Jenny, are you very lonely? Are you very cold and lonely? I did love you, Dad loved you, I loved you, I loved you. He stops. Can anyone hear the words in his moonlit head? Can Jenny? Can God?

He rises and walks on memory feet to the gate of the dead, starts the slow return to the farm. Oh, Jenny, you shouldn't have killed yourself for sadness, it leaves too much behind.

NINE

Days and nights pass pointless now. Jenny's been buried one week, two . . . Only David and his Dad share the scar, while Iorweth and his Mam grow closer, more intimate, more knowing.

The morning sun breaks through the tiny panes of the living-room window, which seems to screw its glass eyes smaller to keep out the unfamiliar brightness. Iorweth, standing by the table, a large open Bible in his hand, finds his plain black suit made clownish by the squares of sunlight which dapple him into Dutch patches. Mrs James, in matching black, bobs slowly backwards and forwards in the rocking chair, eyes closed, the world in her ears.

"Therefore as the fire devoureth the stubble, and the flame consumeth the chaff," reads Iorweth, "so their root shall be as rottenness and their blossom shall go up as dust."

"Not so fast, Iorweth," says Mrs James, moving to and fro, a metronome, "not too fast."

"Because they have cast away the law of the Lord of Hosts and despised the Word of the Holy One of Israel . . ."

"Better."

"Therefore is the anger of the Lord kindled against His people and He hath stretched forth His hand against them and hath smitten them and the hills did tremble and their carcasses were torn in the middle of the street."

"Better."

"For all this His anger is not turned away and His hand is stretched out still." A pause. The Bible words float to silence among the sunlit dust.

"Good, very good," says Mrs James, coming to a stop, slowly opening her eyes and letting in the world at last. "You read very well, Iorweth, Mam's pleased." Iorweth closes the Bible, places it on the dresser, then moves through the sun and takes his mother's hand. He kneels beside the rocking chair now and they look into each others' eyes and beyond the eyes into the dark and secret places of the mind where thoughts forget disguise. Closer, more intimate, knowing.

David, sitting half a mile away by the stream, leans back against a tree, feels its gnarled skin press into his shoulders and stares up at the blue of the sky. He knows something too. He knows now that it was Alun Rhys who made Jenny pregnant. Alun Rhys . . . Annie Rhys . . . just names, people who had been born and grown up just a few miles away, but it might as well have been Africa. Over to his left he can see the farmhouse, knows that Mam and Iorweth are in there, in the shadows of it, growing closer with the days. Why closer since the death of Jenny?

On his feet now, brushing away the clinging grass and as the stream gurgles and burbles in Welsh to the stones, he moves quickly away towards the stile, which leads to the lane, which leads to the road, which leads to the village where the Rhyses live. Too many questions bursting in his head, the jigsaw isn't taking shape, there's got to be a start to answers, there's got to be a start right now.

Knocks on the dark green door, steps back and waits. Street children swirl around him with hoops, chattering and screeching, birds after bread. The door opens, Annie stands there and David sees the recognition of him flicker in her eyes before they go dead.

"Yes," she asks, as though he were selling pegs.

"I'm David James."

"Yes, I know."

"Is your brother in?"

"No."

"Do you know where he is?"

"No, he doesn't come in much now. What do you want?"

"I think perhaps he and I ought to have a talk."

"There's nothing to say . . . we're sorry . . . all of us . . . but there's no more to say." She moves to close the door.

"Well, I think there is," says David, coming in close to the door's stone frame, "I think there is." There's anger now in his voice, anger at a world of dead faces.

"Go away, please," says Annie, her eyes souls on sticks. "Leave us be, we've been punished enough."

"Annie . . . can't I come in? Just for a little while?"

"Why?"

"In pity's name, I've got to know what happened."

The street children have moved away slightly to a chalked wall and a snigger bursts from them. They have smelt the tension and like a sudden glimpse of knickers it makes them huddle and giggle.

"You must *know* what happened," says Annie, and her voice is quiet and urgent and wanting to bring down the curtain.

"Only *part* of it," says David, "I want to know it all."

There's another burst of sound from the snigger of children and Annie steps back into the blackness of the hallway and opens the door wide.

"Come in then," she says, "quick."

David steps into the hall, the door closes behind him, shutting out the children and the street and all the unseen eyes watching, trying to put two and two together. He follows Annie down the brown hall and into the cluttered living-room that's ill with years of Chapel and shalt nots. Annie turns quickly and faces him.

"You can't stay long," she says, "they'll be back soon,

54

Mam and Dad." She looks so young in this old room, so alive among the death of clutter. There's something about her . . . like Jenny perhaps?

"What do you want to know?" she asks.

"I'm not sure, how it started perhaps? My brother tells me it was because Jenny thought your brother looked like me . . . does he?"

"Haven't you ever seen him?"

"No."

"Yes, he looks like you and perhaps that's how it started." Annie moves to a corner of the room and sits in a small chair whose stiff black arms grip her waist.

"It began shortly after you went to London," she says, and her voice is low and her eyes look down into her lap. "Alun used to go for walks up the mountains, he saw Jenny there one day. They talked about things, and after that they met quite often. He used to come home all excited. He never showed his excitement to Mam and Dad though, never told them anything, only me he told." She stops, resting her thoughts on her lap, then she goes on.

"Then one evening he came home sad, didn't want to talk, then after a while he told me he'd done something with Jenny."

David stares at the floor and waits.

"Made love with her," says Annie, and her voice is a whisper now and her little body filled with shame, her lap filled with pictures.

On the mound of her left knee birds circle, making no comment. In the folds of her dress Alun and Jenny lie in the long split second before the stroke that makes a deed a fact. A time and place is conjured on flannel for a moment and then breaks.

Annie rises from the embrace of the chair, moves to the window, pulls aside a curtain and looks down the street.

"You'd better go," she says, "perhaps we can talk some other time."

"No, *now*," says David, "what happened after that?"

55

Annie turns from the window, suddenly as defeated as the furniture. "They stopped seeing each other for a long, long time. Then they started up again."

"Why?"

"How do I know *why*? People do these things. Anyway, what was wrong with it? Boys court girls all the time."

"Did your parents know?"

"They knew they were seeing each other, yes, they didn't think it was serious, they had other plans for Alun . . . someone better in mind for him . . . I'm sorry."

"Go on," says David, wading deeper.

"A few months ago he came home after seeing Jenny and just ran upstairs to his bedroom. I went up and listened outside his door; he was crying. I'd never heard him cry before, not ever. I went into the room, sat with him on the bed, hugged him, asked him what was wrong . . . and he told me."

"That Jenny was pregnant."

"Yes."

"Did he tell your parents?"

"No, he was too afraid, but my father found out."

"What did they do when they found out?"

Annie was plucking her dress in the pain of the remembrance. She moves back to the hug of the chair, sits as she sat that night. White and staring and adrift from hope is Alun's face. Mr Rhys stands stiffly in front of him, the cold steel spectacles warmer than the eyes behind them, his skeleton hands caressing a cane.

"Jenny James is pregnant," says Mr Rhys.

"Yes."

Mrs Rhys who had been pretending to read a book closes it, and beckons to Annie to leave the room. They go slowly out as though reluctantly leaving a grave and close the door behind them. They move out into the tiny garden, shuffle about among the sickly flowers. Annie sits on a broken bit of wall and begins to moan.

Her mother, standing in the shadow of some shrubs says, "Stop that row . . . stop it!"

56

Mr Rhys strokes the cane, slowly, rhythmically, an overture to agony.

"Are you responsible?" he asks.

"Dad . . ."

"Are you?"

"Forgive me."

"Are you?"

"Yes."

Scarcely moving his body or arm Mr Rhys whips the cane across Alun's face. Outside Annie hears the swish of the cane and she moans again and her mother, pretending to study a flower says, "Stop it now, Annie."

Alun remains at attention, not a muscle moving, as the blood begins to seep from his nose.

"Forgive me," he says again.

The cane smashes back into his face. Alun feels the blood among his teeth, feels the pain tearing at the nerves behind his eyes, opens his mouth to speak as the blow of the cane splits his lip and forces him finally back against the wall. Tears now, pouring from his aching eyes, mixing with the blood as he raises his hand to ward off the next blow, but the cane whips across his nose, then back across his ear, then bites into his neck. Through the pain and blood and mucus which he can see smearing the floor tiles Alun hears himself crying "Dad . . . Dad . . ." but the beating goes on and on while Annie sits on the wall outside, moaning, and her mother pretends that things are different and Alun's voice, divorced from his personality, is now screaming like an animal.

So that's how it was, and David now stands where Alun stood in pain, and can find no words. Annie is still plucking her dress.

"They could have married, couldn't they?" says David.

"Yes," says Annie, "But Jenny killed herself, didn't she?"

Yes, Jenny killed herself, God Almighty, hung herself in a barn. David opens the door, down the brown hall that seems pleased at his passing, opens the door to the screeching street.

"Don't come again," calls Annie, "please don't come again."

David closes the door and moves off down the hill, past the huddled, wondering cottages, over the hump-back stone bridge, where a boy is fishing with a twig and a piece of string that doesn't even reach the river. Through the village that seems tired with time, and where groups of people who will live and die within a four-mile square, lean and squat and chatter to prove they're there.

Up the rise where the trees stand still, ticking off the seasons, through the rotting five-barred gate, turned into a wooden visitor's book by the penknives of long-ago lovers, and up into the feet of the mountains. On he goes through unfelt miles, his mind in silence, till finally his body shouts its tiredness and he falls back in the coarse grass.

Thinks of Annie, then, in the zombie village, pluck-ing her dress, waiting to grow old and die, like all the others who chatter away the uncomprehended now. Thinks of her looking young in the age of the room, alive among the death, moving in the still, something about her, the way of her . . . Yes, like Jenny . . . or Helen . . .

Helen . . . England . . . London . . . A white butterfly blunders close, beautiful, complete. London . . . Wales . . . the sigh of wind, the laugh of traffic . . . London.

He closes his eyes and listens to the coarse grass blades whispering about him, saying things to each other, to the rocks, to the trees, saying what? He closes his eyes tighter, making fireworks in his head, shutting out the whispers, the Welsh whispers. Silence . . . London . . . London ablaze . . .

TEN

Ablaze is the City of London, ablaze with the illuminations for the Coronation of King George V. David moves among the jostling crowds, pushed, buffeted, he walks and stumbles on, trying to absorb the atmosphere, the Englishness, to shed his skin. On he goes, cutting through the crowds and sounds, down Cockspur Street where the Oceanic House shames the heavens with its thousands of lamps and vast, white electric star. On past the Bank of England where the Old Lady of Threadneedle Street stands preening and proud in her coronation finery.

Stands there while passers-by bump his shoulders and tread on his new black shoes, stands without caring, without feeling, seeing only the red and white lights, the huge gilt wreaths enclosing Royal monograms, crowns glowing with an amber radiance. Flotsam in this new river he floats among the faceless, nameless English, floats among the shouts and laughter and bursting electric brilliance of the night.

Stands gasping and bruised before the North British and Mercantile Insurance Office as it declares its loyalty with a ripple of light from hundreds of fairy lights and blazing crystals. Moves on, breathing in this new world, attempting a new birth, under the festoons of light. Venetian masts stretch in burning salute from Piccadilly to Hyde Park Corner to St James' Street . . . ablaze is the City of London and David, the stranger, drinks it in. But Wales won't let him free as he walks among the fire of celebration.

Won't let him free as he walks through the front door of his new found lodgings and Mrs Shaw, standing cheery by her scrubbed table, and drawing off hot water from the boiler says "Your friend has called to see you . . . whatsisname? . . . Emrys. He's waiting in the parlour, you can talk to him in there if you like."

Down the narrow passage and into the parlour. Emrys, sitting in a red, plush chair, rises and extends a smooth, white hand. "Hello, David," he says.

Won't let him free in the summer-house as the boredom of words beats against his ears, but his eyes see only Helen, the late sun setting behind her shoulders. Soon he's rising and moving to the door.

"What's the matter, David?" asks Emrys, catching him by the arm.

"You," shouts David, "That's what's the matter, the whole bloody lot of you, now let me go." And go he does, while God stops the clocks, on down the path, down the street, and half a mile away he hears a shout and turns and Helen is running towards him, calling his name. They stand for a while and talk then move off together, link hands unexpectedly, and laugh. But Wales hangs about in the London night, watches them go.

Watches them later at the Crystal Palace as they climb the stone steps of the Central Transept and look about them at the wild, romantic, fairy-like appearance of it. Up they go, hand in hand and laughing, to the upper terrace. Look down into the gardens and terraces and into several counties beyond. Look in wonder and young delight at the close-cropped lawns, the six fountains ranged along the Grand Terrace, water temples sixty feet high made of ornamental ironwork and richly gilded.

They run and dodge and swerve among the thousands of others, stumbling, giggling, feeling alone in their wonderful madness as the fountains cascade about them.

Burst with colour do the gardens as they skip and dance like jesters down the winding walks and slopes of the English landscape garden. Then they sit, holding their sides with stitch, and look beyond, where in the distance the churches of Bromley, Beckenham and Penge can be clearly seen.

David sits on a wooden bench, lets his head loll back. "So this is it," he says, "Crystal Palace."

"This is it," says Helen, sitting by him.

"I can't believe it, it's too crazy."

They both laugh again. It's easy laughing today and Helen moves closer to him and their legs touch and almost their lips and David quickly breaks away and pretends to look with interest at the ornamental fountains down in the Italian Garden.

"What's the matter, David?"

"Nothing, nothing's the matter."

There's plenty the matter though, and his inside is churning with a sort of fear. Helen is luring him to commitment and he's not ready, not ready yet, not ready.

"David, what is it? Tell me, what's the matter with you?"

Good question, Helen, but David can't answer, even if he knew the answer, so they stand together in stillness, suddenly aware of the other thousands seething like excited ants and adding their own noise and colour to the day. Then Helen smiles, wise girl, and says, "Come on then, let's see the rest of the place."

She moves away, deliberately not taking his hand this time, and David, smiling now, moves too beside her and they walk off into the luxuriance and style of the place, walk off among the ghosts of the Romans and Greeks, and all the time Wales watches them go.

Watches them through the following weeks as they sit in his lodgings and talk of the theatre and fashion. Watches David struggle with his inner devils as Helen watches too on the outside of his agony.

Weeks into months and David desperately drinking

London finds Wales on his heels as the newspapers tell of the riots there.

"Read all about it," calls the news-seller, his voice cracking out like metal from just above the mound of grey scarf. David buys a paper, reads, and Wales comes at him, up out of the print.

The railway lines lie still, untroubled by the usual beating of wheels. Bits of paper drift over the bored track, empty cardboard boxes blow in the wind, miserable. Trucks, blown to pieces by explosives, stand in fragments, looking shocked. A goods shed, turned skeleton, smoulders still, after the attention of men inflamed by stolen drink and injustice.

On the embankment rioters sit in groups like dark flowers, pelt stones at the soldiers who stand and watch, and wait. A soldier fires, the crack of the report sends a cat daft by a dustbin, then more shots. The black flowers stir, uneasy. One man sits on a garden wall, passive, watching, his face twitches as the shots start.

"Read all about it," cries the London voice, and David reads on.

"Don't worry," cries someone in the crowd, "they're only using blanks." The men laugh again, and pelt stones again and the shots ring out again. The man sitting passive on the garden wall falls back dead among the plants and old tin cans in the garden. A small silence now, a baby yelling somewhere, more shots. Running now is a man in his Sunday best, runs to the shelter of a wrecked truck, shouts out "Christ, they're real bullets." More shots, confusion, and others fall, in the final pain.

Hours later brown soldiers form in the grey of early Sunday morning and advance into the crowds with bayonets drawn. Screams in Llanelly, and coughs silenced in the House of Commons as Winston Churchill rises to say "To prevent wholesale looting it was necessary to use military forces of the Crown with the utmost promptitude."

"Read all about it."

Oh yes, there's London, there's Helen, the passing of

two years. Continuous trips to Richmond and the peace and difference of the river. Punts guided by slender young men dressed in white, their straw boaters at jaunty angles. Women lolling back in the punts like overtended orchids, their parasols making giant water lilies on the surface. There's talk of war, of course, but not too deep, so the men in formal dress stand on the banks of the river and watch the women mimic summer in the colour of their costumes and the fruit and feathers of their hats. David and Helen sit back, let the river go by as they sip tea, but Wales watches them at this start of 1914.

David walks along the streets of London on his way to his job at Aplin's the draper. Moves quicker as though to kick Wales off his heels . . . but it's there in his blood, in his skin, in his brain, in his soul. Years have passed, but it's there. What in God's name is it about Wales? What terrible primeval power seems to lurk in the place?

The buildings of London blur and burst about him. He moves on, quicker, through the unseen, unheard people. He must talk, talk to Emrys, kill or coax the ghost in his heart. Faster, bumping, shoving, past his place of work, jogging, swaying on a tram that carries him out of the smoke and bustle and soon there's a quiet, tree-lined street. Legs going faster, faster, must talk to Emrys, at least talk. Knocks at the door, waits while a bird chirps the seconds of his impatience, then the door opens and in its shadow Emrys stands, looking flushed, dishevelled, his shirt flowing over the top of his trousers like water over a weir.

"Hello, old boy," says Emrys, his voice cool in the heat of himself. "What brought *you* here?"

"Who is it?" says Helen's voice from the depths of the hall.

Helen? Pushes past Emrys now, does David, stares in disbelief at Helen standing there. Her face too is flushed, her clothes adrift with excitement. A silence. Helen turns and moves away into the front room. Emrys affects a pose, leaning against the wallpaper.

"You haven't answered my question," he says, trying to look as though love had been the last thing going on, "what brought you here?"

David stands on the edge of sickness, the thick pile of the carpet licking his ankles. Turns and goes out, down the path, opens the gate, hears Emrys give a sudden burst of laughter from the house, walks in deadness up the tree-lined street.

"Of course I've been seeing Emrys."

"But I thought you'd finished with him?"

"I did, it started again."

"Why?"

"Do you really have to . . ."

"Yes."

She moves ungainly around the room, as though seeking words in the furniture, under the cushions.

"He makes me feel wanted."

"Don't I?"

"I can't live on talk, David."

"What?"

"You've never touched me the whole time we've known each other. You know what I mean."

"In heaven's name, Helen, is that all you're . . ."

"No . . . but it's important."

"You're talking like a whore."

"You know I'm not."

"Well, then . . ."

"But what are *you*?"

"I don't understand."

She takes his arm, firm, hard, hurting him by the elbows. "David, I don't *like* Emrys."

"Ha!"

"I don't . . . it's you I want . . . don't you understand?"

"No, I don't."

Helen moves close to him, each inch of her a challenge, a promise, a dare. On the threshold of threat she gazes deep into the eyes of him, then steps back. Slowly and

64

theatrically she removes her satin dress. David, in a world gone mad, watches, and to his surprise feels lust, like too much food in the pit of his stomach. She lies back on the bed wearing only knickers and stockings, begins to writhe.

"Come on, David."

He pulls off his jacket and tie, kicks off his shoes, stands there in hell. Real hell too, with ogres and brimstone and Mam standing in the glow of the childhood bedroom door.

"Come on, now," says Mam. "Time you two were asleep."

"Come on," says Helen. "Come on, love, it'll be all right, really, really." She scrambles from the bed and her hands tear at the buttons on his flies.

"Come on, come on." Her mouth goes closer and David moans the devil from his mind, his fingers in her hair, scratching at her scalp.

Mam moves gracefully to Iorweth's bed, bends down, slow, loving, places her lips on his forehead, kisses with a world of love. "Goodnight, boy," she says, then goes out, leaving David untouched and alone.

His hand goes up Helen's leg to the top of the stocking, the bed groans with them, flesh at the top of the stocking, Helen shouting as though being burned, his trousers fall away in the sweat and struggle and gasping, fall away, slide from the eiderdown and break their legs on the floor. Tongues in each other's mouths, licking, sucking, drinking . . . and then the letter on the table by the door and Helen waiting, the sweat cooling on her body like the start of death. . . .

A drunk sings outside. The door closes. David standing without his trousers, the letter glued to his hand, knows she has gone for ever. Helen, Jenny, gone for ever. Puts on his trousers, then, to hide his shame in serge, and stop the ogres hissing in his head. Moves to the window, pulls back the curtain, sees Helen walking in the orange light of the street, walking away into the bricks of the city. Sits on the bed, feels the cooling heat of the sheets, looks down at the crumpled letter in his hand . . . Jenny dead.

The coarse grass blades stab his cheek, his eyes open. The butterfly is still close. He looks past it, up to the blue of the sky, remembers Daniel saying "I sometimes wonder what God's playing at." God? There's no God, doesn't exist, no doubt of it. Rises then, scuffs through the dry grass up to the higher level where Wales is wider and a gentle wind floats above the heat bringing promises. On he goes, higher, slower, till he reaches the top and stands there like a beacon.

If only he could keep rising, flying, climbing upwards. Height is an escape, a drug. There's light up there, and silence, but the peace is temporary and dangerous. The mind aching for peace finds only the kiss of stupidity. Those who live on heights wear the look of vacancy, their souls have been sold to the wind and cloud and quiet. There's no escape, things are as they are, a few miles down in the huddle of the village Annie Rhys is still plucking her dress in pain.

So he stands there, does David, gulping in the cold as though it were a cure for things, stands there crippled by a God that doesn't exist. Stands there, looking without seeing, standing in silence, the tears starting.

ELEVEN

Alun Rhys stands alone in a field. His days are spent in walking and thinking, though sometimes he walks without thinking and the miles and hours are eaten up by silence. That's the best of all for him, the time that passes without being felt. Down the lane he goes, hands in pocket, chin on chest, not seeing the hedges or smelling them, or hearing the echo of his footsteps like a knock in the hill.

Into the cemetery he walks, among the earth and flowers, stones and mounds that seem to heave with death. The ground seems alive and bubbling, almost unable to contain the generations of dead. He remembers going to school one day and suddenly freezing in his tracks. A giant cockroach is plodding blackly and satanically across the path. The thing exudes foulness, grossness, it plops with deadliness and blight. In instinctive horror Alun stamps his foot on it and from the burst black belly of it dozens of little cockroaches scatter wildly in the sudden light. One day, he feels, this cemetery will do that, the heaving, yawning earth will crack its crust and throw up its dead. Then like a scum mark on a bath after the water has gone, the ground will be covered by the startled skeletons, the half bodies, the ghosts and shades and shapes, some of them screaming in a warm, sick despair of non-Heaven and some of them laughing in a sound that only the soul will recognise, remember, though from God knows where, or when.

He kneels by Jenny's grave, as David had done, kneels and stares hard at the soil. Stares as though his eyes could pierce the surface, cut through the clay and see Jenny lying there, wasting away in her wooden house. He should have gone to the funeral, he knows it, but knows too that even if his parents had allowed it he wouldn't have gone. Jenny running and laughing on a hill was one thing, Jenny being put into the ground was something else, something that couldn't be faced.

Alun rises, moves away from the grave, moves among the sad crosses, facing things is terrible hard. Not only facing Jenny, or what remains of her, but also facing his family, and facing David. He'd like to talk to David, discuss, explain, but there's no way to start. So his days are spent in walking, and thinking, and not thinking, and studying David from a distance. Studies him now, sees him half a mile away, sees him standing in the yard of the farm leaning against the barn like a little ladder.

David straightens up and crosses the yard to where his father is ankle deep in hens, spraying grain about him.

"They're looking fine," says David.

"Happiest hens in the county, boy," says Mr James, and another shower of grain rains down on the hens as they cluck and peck and strut in a feathered riot.

"See that one there?" goes on Mr James, pointing to a fat hen wobbling near a broken cart wheel, spokes filled with cobwebs. "That's Bronwen, that is. She's my favourite, lays eggs like boulders, does Bronwen. Pass me that bucket, will you, boy?"

David hands the bucket to his father and Mr James with a little laugh sprays more grain among the excited, colliding hens. Well, why shouldn't they be excited when food falls from the skies? Peck, peck, peck, a way to pass time, and God, when you're a hen a way to pass time is something to get excited about.

"Is anything wrong, boy?" asks Mr James, knowing there is, but disguising his worry in concentration on grain.

"Why do you ask?"

"I just mean you've been hovering around me all day . . . like a shadow . . . only at a distance. Every time I've turned round I've seen you standing a little way off . . . watching."

David leans an elbow on the broken cart wheel, his hand by accident tearing a cobweb. He wipes away the strands on his jacket.

"Dad . . . can we go for a walk?"

"What? . . . Just you and me?"

"Yes, just you and me."

"Well, I'm pretty busy as a matter of fact."

"Please, Dad."

"Why, boy? . . . What's on your mind?"

"I just want to go walking with you . . . like we used to long ago."

Long ago. The sound of the words turns Mr James' stomach sick with sadness and he smiles, a whistle in the dark smile.

"All right, boy, all right," he says, turning the bucket upsidedown and letting the last of the grain drift down among the feathers. "We'll go walking. You'll have to wait a bit though, hour or two."

"That's fine," says David.

Mr James clangs the bucket down on a piece of concrete, knows he's opened a door to danger. The challenge has been made, the duel will take place.

In the distance, unseen by Mr James and David, Alun Rhys pulls back from his screen of bramble and lopes off among the dips and rises. What had David and his father been saying to each other? What words did they use? There's so much to say to everybody, but fear pegs the words before they start. Anyway, what words do you use? And is it words that are wanted or understanding without words? Everybody is behaving, nobody is being, they're trapped and too crippled to use the key. Everybody's dancing, but there isn't any music.

There's music, though, later, in the mountains as David and Mr James begin the slow climb. The wind strikes notes out of the angles of rock while the leaves of the trees shhhh the noise. The grass blades part to let the wind through and from a distance the fields are turned to sea, and the waves of wind glide across the acres and break against the foot of the mountain. Above, puffs of dark cloud drift slowly, then link together, forming a giant black candyfloss which settles and waits on the horizon. There's a biting freshness in the air, a taste of rain, and the weak sun paints the countryside in water colours.

Birds, like black dots, lie on the wind and take free rides above the valley and up the side of Craig Point, where sheep stand stupid, feeling the beginnings of storm in their wool. Mr James puffs to a halt.

"Let's sit here for a while, boy," he says. "Rest my old legs. I'm getting old, David, Old Father Time is nibbling at my bones."

They sit together on a little ledge of stone and look down to where the farmhouse is small enough to put in your hand.

"Threatening rain again," says Mr James. They look about them at the troubled sky, then David says

"It hasn't rained since we buried Jenny."

"I found her Teddy bear in the attic yesterday," says Mr James. "Funny old thing, it is, but when she was younger she wouldn't go anywhere without it. She'd tuck it under her arm and run across the fields to the stream and sit there for hours talking to it. Yes . . . funny old thing. The dog chewed its legs off. I told her I'd make some new legs for it . . . never did."

"Stop it now, Dad."

"Still, didn't matter . . . little Jenny . . . oh dear."

"Stop it now."

Mr James smiles to break his sadness and slaps his hands on his knees.

"Oh, but it's nice up here," he says, "nice and fresh and far away. Look at Craig Point winking in that bit of sunshine."

"And the wind singing songs in the mountains."

"That's it," laughs Mr James, "that's it . . . you've

remembered. How many times when you were a boy have we stood around here and looked down into the valley and said 'Listen to the wind singing songs in the mountains'? I didn't think you'd remember that. They were wonderful days. Do you remember the winter we had the very deep snow?"

"And you made a sledge."

"That's it," laughs Mr James, rocking happily in the remembrance, "a big sledge for two."

"And we painted it green." David's remarks are cold, like statements, facts at the trial. "And the paint came off on our clothes."

"And Mam said 'Couple of silly children, that's what you are'."

"And the snowman on Blackberry Ridge," says David, "he had eyes of coal and a carrot nose."

"That's right . . . we called it Mr Garfield."

"Because it looked like Mr Garfield, the English doctor."

"It did, it did," shouts Mr James, bouncing in an unexpected happiness. "Boy, that was a wonderful snowman. It seems a long time ago."

"A long time."

Mr James stares ahead, lost in the warmth of his memories. Then he lets the cosy comfort drain away and he faces David.

"You've grown into a fine lad, David, a fine lad . . . but . . . well . . . some nights when I'm lying in bed and it's dark I wish hard that we could go back through the years and there'd be you and me again, younger and silly, laughing in the snow."

David doesn't answer, he just looks down at his shoes, remains unmoving, ungiving.

"Take no notice, boy," says Mr James, "the ravings of a man getting past it. Things change . . . people change . . . snowmen melt."

He gets to his feet, gives a little stretch, his shirt climbs over the top of his belt and shows the grey brown of his vest.

"I suppose Wales seems dull to you now."

"Dull?"

"Well, after London and everything."

"I've told you, I don't like it there."

"You'll get used to it, give it time."

"I want to be here."

"Now, David," says Mr James, thrusting his hands into the pits of his pockets, "you're young, don't waste your youth on trees and sky. There's nothing here but breathing and waiting, nowhere for the brain to grow."

"What do you suggest I do?"

"Do? You can fly, boy, fly like the wind."

"There's no point," says David, rising and moving slightly away to a clump of ferns. "The further I run the nearer I am to home. All I want is for Mam . . ."

Comes in closer now, does Mr James, turns David by the shoulder. "Mam . . . Mam . . . can't you talk of anything else? Can't your eyes see another place? Another life? Can't you see green grass on other hills? Sunshine on other fields?"

"I'm me, Dad, no one else."

"Maybe the grass isn't greener on the other side of the hill, maybe it isn't, but it's different, David, and that's all I've ever wanted from life, different grass under my feet."

"Dad, I'm *me*," says David, breaking free from his father's grip, "you can't live your life through me."

"What are you saying? What tommy-rot are you saying?"

"I'm not a younger you, that's all."

"I never said that."

"You have, in a hundred different ways, you've said it."

"Oh, come on now, boy. All I want is for you to be happy, believe me, that's all I want."

"I believe you."

"We're alike, David, we're the same."

"And that's the trouble."

"Trouble?"

"That's why I'm punished as well as you, I'm punished for what you did."

Mr James steps back a bit, peers into David's eyes, feeling frightened of the knowledge there.

"What do you mean? I don't understand."

"At least I have an understanding now why Mam has treated me the way she has. It helps, Dad, it helps to know."

"Know what?" asks Mr James, and with that question he enters the mire of misery, and makes his laughter of a few minutes ago something from another life that's suddenly over.

"Tell me about the girl in Cardiff," says David.

TWELVE

Above Craig Point the birds are riding the wind in gliding swoops of boredom. Slowly, with no care or knowledge of time they drift in silent arcs above the two who are peeling each other to bits.

"What did you say?" asks Mr James.

"The girl in Cardiff, Dad."

"Who told . . . ?"

"Tell me about her, Dad, tell me how it was, tell me about her."

Turns, does Mr James, a lion sick of the whip, and moves blindly off for peace.

"I'm going back," he says, "are you coming?"

"All right," shouts David, and his voice bounces about the grey rocks, growing greyer with waiting for storm. "All right, go back, go back to pretending and whistling in the dark. Don't care, walk in a fog and dream your dreams. Let the thoughts stay silent, the lips unkissed, the words unspoken, don't care."

He stumbles after his father, yelling louder in his helplessness. "You say all you want is my happiness, yet you let me suffer, you won't explain."

Mr James turns suddenly, his boots kicking up a cloud of dust which clings about him.

"You think explaining will help?" he yells back.

"I don't know."

"You think it will change things?"

74

"I don't know," says David, coming in close among the clinging dust. "I only know I'm twenty-five and the snowman days are over."

They stand close, facing each other, their clothes and skin coated white with dust. David sees his Dad grow old in front of him and almost die inside his clothes.

"Don't hate me, David."

"I don't."

"I couldn't bear it if you hated me."

"Dad . . ."

"Couldn't bear it, boy."

David slumps on to a rock seat. "I don't hate you, Dad," he says, and the words are quiet and simple and tired. Mr James sits beside him and for a moment they share a silence and David feels the first drop of rain glance off the bridge of his nose.

"Now," says David, "just tell me about the girl in Cardiff and about Mam and Iorweth."

"And if I don't tell you?"

"Then there won't be any love anywhere, Dad, not anywhere."

"Who told you about Cardiff?"

"It doesn't matter, does it, Dad?"

"No," says Mr James, long and slow and feeling a raindrop touch a knuckle, "no, it doesn't matter, nothing matters now, does it?" He waits, letting the words come unwilling from the shadows of himself.

"All right, then, all right, if you must know, if it matters to you, if it makes a difference."

The birds are still gliding, lower now as the sky moves down.

"Well, it was nothing much, the girl in Cardiff, I mean, just a girl, not even pretty, just a girl. You see, boy, your Mam loved me very much, too much, but I didn't feel . . ."

He closes his eyes tight in the pain of memory, and in the red and blackness of his head he is young and a stream bustles about in the sunshine. There is a half-submerged tambourine, strangely out of place in the tangle of weeds, agitated by the stream's fever and making now a tinkling island for a duck.

He looks up from the diamonds on the water's surface and sees a young and beautiful girl on the opposite bank. She smiles at him, slow, as though she's known him a thousand years and the moment is only a fragment in a long-planned pattern. Now, barefoot, she paddles across the stream and comes to beside him.

"Hello," she says.

"Hello," he says back, feeling foolish a bit and staring at his toes.

"My name's Alice, Alice Owen."

"Mine's James, Robert James."

"Yes, I know."

"How?"

"I asked."

"Oh."

She moves around him, as though assessing something she was going to buy. She is saying something as she circles, about where she works, about how she's been watching him for some time, about how she knows he helps his father to run a farm, but his head is buzzing with the suddenness of things and the water is sparkling pain into his eyes. Then she's suddenly paddling back across the stream, her feet breaking the diamonds and she's calling out "I'll see you another time, Robert."

She does, too. For weeks and months, and then one day, with a drizzle forcing them to shelter under a rock canopy she kisses him fully on the lips. He leaps up, shocked, and bangs his head on the rock, and she laughs and kisses him again.

"Alice," he says and his voice is wrapped in anger. "There was no call for that, no call." He attempts to stand upright, dignified, with his head bursting, but she pulls him down on to his knees and her lips are on his again. Soon the drizzle clears and they move out into the damp and crumpled countryside. She takes his hand in hers and there's a look in her eyes that tells of something inside of her, something he doesn't feel. She runs ahead

76

of him, twirling, spinning, pirouetting, shouting out her happiness and inside his heart he hears the clang of the trap loud enough to waken the souls of the Druids sleeping in the stones and oak trees.

Mr James opens his eyes, sees the fat raindrops staining a nearby leaf, feels David's eyes pulling the talk out of him. "All the same," he says, "I married her, married her without loving her, don't know why, not really, but . . . well . . . there was no one else and . . . Well, we moved to this farm and shortly afterwards you were born and then a few years later, Jenny, and for a while we seemed set . . . and that was the trouble."

He waits, for a moment feeling the memory of that time, feeling the suffocation of the days.

"I didn't like being set, you see, stuck with a woman I didn't love."

He stops again, just stares, still, not feeling the lifeless wind swirl without strength around him, spitting rain.

"Then one day, when I was in Cardiff," he says, and David leans closer and listens harder to the words which are coming quieter and more mechanical. "On business, and I met this girl, can't remember her name, but we got talking and, well, she invited me back to her room and we . . . well . . . it was just something different . . . greener grass. Then afterwards, when I left her, she was, like, crying and later she tried to get in touch with me and, well, your Mam found out what had happened. She knew, of course, that ever since we'd been married I'd had no love for her and she'd come to accept it in a sort of way, but this was something different, something different. She didn't flare at me, she wasn't angry, she just seemed to die inside."

Die inside . . . Mr James has died inside and even the wind finally shivers to silence among the bushes and the rain comes more steady.

"And when I touched her," says Mr James, reaching out a hand now in remembrance, "it was like touching stone . . . and there were no words."

"And Iorweth?" says David the prompter.

77

"Oh, what's the point, boy?"

"And Iorweth?"

Mr James lets out a long, sad sigh, studies his hands and listens to the first low rumble of thunder along the horizon beyond Craig Point.

"Well," he says finally. "Her way of punishing me was to go away for a while and, well, when she came back she was pregnant. I never knew who the man was, I pretended not to care." Mr James rises, looking terrible, old and ill within his skin, the rain putting little rivers down his face. He stares long and hard down into the valley, down to where the farm is, down to where *she* is, the spider at the centre. The words come faster now.

"I just watched her grow, month by month, and become somebody different, somebody cold and unloving, and different. We never talked or touched, we ate and slept in silence. Iorweth was the baby, of course, and from the time he was born she heaped love on him, mountains of love. You, me and Jenny were forgotten, we were on one side, Mam and Iorweth on the other. It broke my heart, boy, to see you and Jenny growing up, wondering, crying. Now Jenny's dead, she's dead, she's dead because she let somebody love her."

He tears his face away from the valley, moves a little to the right, then left, someone going nowhere, and shouts out, "Now it's told, now it's told."

"Now it's told," says David, dead and flat.

"I'm the one to blame, aren't I? Me to blame?"

"Yes."

"Oh, David, boy, I'm sorry."

"Let's go back, now."

"I'm sorry."

"Let's go back."

"You asked me to say."

"Yes."

"You asked me to tell you, you wanted me to . . ."

"Yes."

"David, don't look . . ."

78

"Let's go back now, Dad."

David moves away, walking fast in the rain, and all around them Nature is rustling. Down the edge of the mountain they go, separate.

Therefore as the fire devoureth the stubble and the flame consumeth the chaff, so their root shall be as rottenness and their blossom shall go up as dust.

"David!" called Mr James, stumbling in his son's wake, "David!"

David, though, is deaf to words now, he just walks faster, firmer, deader, putting a distance between them that nothing will ever close. Coldly, cruelly, he makes a wound with space.

Therefore is the anger of the Lord kindled against his people and He hath stretched forth His hand against them and hath smitten them, and the hills did tremble.

Mr James stops, gasping, the rain and sweat stinging his eyes. He leans, hopeless, on the corpse of a tree and the thunder rumbles nearer, and the birds at last go quiet.

"David!" he cries out again, "David . . . for God's sake, you asked me to tell you, you *asked* me, you *asked* me."

THIRTEEN

Night now, and the storm, matured, hisses its way into every crack and crevice of the farm and shakes in anger against the living-room window. In an island of light from the flickering oil lamp David sits, pretending to read, while Iorweth observes him from the rocking chair and is poised for questions. David flips an unread page, the sound of it crackling lively in the nervous silence, and the new page, too, is only a blur, somewhere to rest his presence while his thoughts are wandering. Iorweth leans in closer and the shadow of him grows and spreads sudden like an ink stain, his hand stretching up the wall and spilling over the ceiling.

"You're very quiet tonight, David," he says.

"Yes."

"Is it the storm making you quiet?"

"Perhaps."

"You went for a walk with Dad today, didn't you?"

"Yes."

"High up in the mountains?"

"Yes."

"Talking were you?"

"Of course."

"Talking about what?"

"It makes no matter."

Iorweth lolls back in the rocking chair and smiles, relaxed, and the black shadow of him shrinks to normal and leans in folds against the dresser. Outside a dog barks wetly and the window has a spasm again like a glass drumskin. Iorweth strokes a finger-nail and says, casual,

"When are you leaving us?"

"When I choose."

"Jenny's buried," says Iorweth, pushing back a bit of skin on the nail, "there's nothing to stop for."

"You'd like to see the end of me, wouldn't you? For good?"

"Yes."

"And the end of Dad."

"Yes. Just Mam and me, that's all I want, all I need . . . all she needs, too."

"Supposing I don't go?"

Iorweth leans forward, his face stone dead. "You'll go," he says.

"There'll still be Dad."

"He'll go in time, that's the way it will be. The weakness and sin will go from the house."

David laughs sudden, like a rifle crack, rises and moves around his chair, jerking like a puppet in his joy.

"You think *I'm* a sinner?" he says, incredulous.

"You're the flesh of a sinner, the seed of weakness."

"Oh, grow up, man," says David, serious now, turning his back on his brother and moving to the dresser where the china plates rattle with his movement. He spins round and shouts:

"If you must spew up the cant do it from a mountain top. I'm sick of the sound, my ears are filled with the poison. All this because of a silly bitch in Cardiff? A stupid five-minute tumble?"

He knows he is asking himself the questions too, but he knows he'll only find out what he's thinking if he hears himself talking. Iorweth rises, pulling his shadow up with him.

"A five-minute tumble?" he says, and the deadness drops from his face, snow in a thaw. "That five-minute tumble cracked Mam's heart and turned her brain to stone. He killed her, Dad killed her, as sure as with a knife. A warm God-fearing woman, destroyed by a stupid man no better than a beast. She gave him love and he mocked her with sin. Broke her like a twig because he didn't love her and since that day there's been darkness in this house."

"You're a fool, Iorweth, a damn fool."

There's a sudden smash of thunder that sounds as though it's exploded in the orchard and the plates start dancing again.

"Iorweth James, the unlovely Christ, passing his terrible judgements. You're mad, Iorweth, mad and evil and I'm sick of you. Cold, dark Iorweth, the cuckoo in the nest, unwanted, unloved, conceived in hate."

"You think I don't know about my birth?" shouts Iorweth, moving in sudden and forcing David back against the dancing plates. "You think I don't know?"

David gives ground to Iorweth's anger and his back touches the dresser, tilting one of the plates to the floor. His feet crunch in the broken china as Iorweth keeps at him.

"You think Mam hasn't told me? You think you're the bearer of terrible news? Is it terrible not to be the seed of a sinner? I've known for years . . . but you warming yourself on Dad's attention, you stumbling in the dark, *you* who didn't know."

David, undignified, scrambles back from Iorweth, collides with the piano, sees their shadows stretching and shrinking up the walls like black elastic ghosts. Iorweth jabs out a finger, shouts,

"How do you feel now, David? How do you feel now? Now you're standing in the light?"

"*You* talk of sinners," says David, still incredulous. "You who burn everything you touch with hate?"

"How do you feel?" goes on Iorweth, his finger jabbing like a dagger. "How do you feel about your father?"

David pauses, his hands pressing into the years of polish on the piano lid, pauses, then says,

"I love and . . ."

"Lies," yells Iorweth, "all lies, David. The light has blinded you, hasn't it? The sockets are empty. Your Dad has given you years of pain. You've had to pay the price as well as he. He cost you Mam's love . . . he . . . and now you know the reason. How do you feel? How?"

Another pause. David opens his mouth, waits for words to come, hears himself say,

"Nothing . . . I feel nothing."

"The love is dead, isn't it?"

"I don't know."

Then Iorweth, too, moves in close to the piano, stands close by David and the long ago picnic people who smile deadly in the gilt frame. Jabs out his white dagger finger again.

"Don't know," he says. "Oh, come on, David, the schooldays are over, you're not a little boy laughing in the snow. Your Dad has shrunk, hasn't he? And the love's dead, isn't it? Isn't it?"

"Iorweth . . ."

"Isn't it? Isn't it?"

Iorweth's question, like an earwig, enters David's head and wriggles blindly and painfully round the brains of him. Iorweth is close and waiting and smiling and there's nothing but hurt.

"Isn't it?" he says again, and the earwig slips and slides.

"Shut up!!" screams David, tearing through the hurt, and moving desperate towards the door. Flings it open now, stands there, absorbing the edge of the storm like blotting paper, then moves out among it. He's heard himself talking, he knows what he thinks.

Stands outside now, in the black and crack of thunder, hears a voice hanging bodyless in the rain.

"David?"

David peers through the curtain of moisture, sees his Dad, covered in a cape, move to beside him,

"Oh, hello, Dad, what are you doing out here?"

"Just checking on things. With the storm and every-

83

thing there's bound to be damage. God, boy, don't stand out here, you'll get soaked to the skin."

"Yes . . . yes . . . well, I'll get inside then," he says, feeling foolish in his wetness.

"That's it," says Mr James.

"Goodnight." David turns towards the shelter of the door. Mr James suddenly moves with him and takes him by the arm. David feels the cold wetness of his suit, hears his Dad say

"David . . ."

"Yes?"

"Why did you make me tell that story today, about the girl?"

"I had to know."

"It's made things worse."

"It's made things clearer."

"You shouldn't have asked me, shouldn't have made me tell it."

"I wanted to know."

"*You! You!*" Mr James is all spray and anger. "Is that all you care about? Hell, boy, I've never hurt you, never deliberately hurt you and yet you hurt me. When you weigh everything up, what difference has it made?"

"I know why things are as they are, that's the difference."

"But does it help matters?" asks Mr James, "does it *help matters?*"

Mr James moves away, his cape cracking about him, disappears into the night and storm. David, past caring of wetness, goes after him, shouts out

"It helps *me.*"

"Is that all you can say to me?" calls Mr James, somewhere over to the left.

"Yes, that's all I can say."

For a moment there is only the sound of the rain, then the voice through it.

"David, you're all I've got—don't turn against me."

"It's not a question of . . ."

"I'm sorry, boy, sorry for everything."

84

David waits for more, tries to see his father, but there's neither sight nor further sound of him. He turns and begins walking back to the dim glow of the farm. A few steps he takes and then his father's voice stops him.

"I wish to Heaven things could have been different," shouts Mr James, still hiding in the night. "I wish to Heaven."

David moves on towards the farm, feeling his father's voice pulling at his back.

"David . . ."

"I'm going inside."

"Get away from here, David, far away. Make a life for yourself."

"Everyone wants me to go."

"Don't be like me."

David reaches the doorway again, stands drowned-ratted in the shelter of it, stares out, a final look into the black, sees now a little firefly of light from his father's storm lamp, hears the voice from by the light.

"I love you, David."

David doesn't answer. He just opens the door and goes inside, stands in the choking stuffiness of it. Iorweth is back in the rocking chair, creaking to and fro, smiling at David's wetness.

"I'm going to bed," says David, moving out of the flickering room, leaving Iorweth still rocking, creaking, knowing. Up the staircase, past his sleeping Mam, into the bedroom. Stands in the dark of it, feeling chilled and ill, wonders about Dad out there in the night, hears the mind moaning around the stones and tiles like an old Welsh wolf.

Drapes his shirt and jacket over the chair, hangs his trousers over the end of the bed where they hang like crumpled cripples' legs. Lies back, lets the bed envelop him in cold, sends out a silent prayer for sleep, which quickly and surprisingly comes, leaving unfinished a thought and picture of Helen standing with her face flushed, her clothes adrift, and Emrys affecting a pose against the hall wallpaper.

FOURTEEN

David's eyes open on blackness, he lies still, listening to the storm still stroking the house. How long has it been? Iorweth stirs in his bed, the springs bending their backs and groaning. Questions click . . . quick . . . what time is it? How long has Iorweth been in bed? Is he awake? Asleep?

"Iorweth?" says David, his voice low and cracked with the remains of sleep.

"What?"

"I was wondering if you were asleep."

"Why?"

"Have you heard Dad come in?"

"No."

"Nor me."

"What are you worrying about? He'll have a lot of fences to check on Craig Point."

"It must be terrible there tonight, he should have waited."

Iorweth humps about in the bed, the springs, old and tired with the years, groan again, slaves in a galley ship.

"If you're so worried why don't you go and see if he's all right?"

David thinks it over, hears the night outside, feels the seduction of the blankets holding him down, melting his thoughts.

"No," he says, as sleep mushrooms inside him, "he'll manage."

"Are you sure," asks Iorweth from the dark opposite. "You sure?"

The earwig questions again.

"Yes, I'm sure."

"Well, that's all right then, isn't it?" says Iorweth, giving a final hump among the springs. "Goodnight."

David lies with his eyes open, wide blind eyes holding in thoughts behind them, listens to Iorweth's breathing grow slowly lower, hears the ghosts stir among the woodwork, feels the blankets getting heavier, warmer, putting gloves on his senses, pulling down the eyelids, black into black.

From a thousand miles away a voice says "David" and then again, nearer, "David . . . wake up."

David opens his eyes, shadows and shapes, bits of dream falling away, sees Iorweth standing by the bed, holding a storm lamp.

"Ummm? . . . Wha . . . ? Iorweth, you're dressed . . . what is it? It's still dark . . . what's happened?"

Iorweth sits tired on David's bed, rests the storm lamp on his knee.

"I woke up," he says. "You were sleeping . . . I let you sleep."

David notices now the wetness of Iorweth, sees the seal shimmer of his oilskins in the light.

"You're wet through," he says, sitting up. "Where have you been?"

"Out, at Craig Point."

David waits, then asks it.

"Dad? . . . Is he back?"

"It's terrible out there," says Iorweth, and his voice shows the fire has gone from him and he's strangely dead.

"Iorweth . . . what the hell has been happening?"

"I went out in the storm, went to look for him, see what had happened."

"And?"

"I found him at Craig Point . . . he must have slipped."

"Slipped?"

"In the storm . . . so dark . . . and the weather . . . didn't see him at first . . . just something huddled."

David is out of the bed now, the clothes spilling about his feet.

"Why didn't you take me with you?"

"There's nothing you could have done."

"Is he hurt bad?"

"He's dead."

David feels the breath sucked out of him and thrown away. Stands, stupid, waiting for his voice.

"Where is he now?" he asks at last.

"Out there," replies Iorweth flatly. "Still out there."

David moves towards his suit, almost overbalancing as the blankets wrap around his feet. He kicks them free and begins dressing in frantic silence, feeling the still wet clothes seep chill about him.

"What are you doing?" asks Iorweth.

"What the hell do you think I'm doing? . . . I'm going out there."

"There's nothing you can do."

"We can't just leave him there," David says, searching for his shoes in the shadows. "We've got to bring him home. Put the oil lamp on, I can't see."

Iorweth wades through the tangle of bedclothes and lights the bedroom lamp. David sees a hiding shoe and grabs it.

"I'm not going out there again," says Iorweth, "not in this weather."

"Suit yourself," says David, moving to the door. "Where is he?"

"At the foot, under the fencing, not far from the north path."

"Right."

Iorweth goes after him, grabs him by the shoulders, spins him round.

"Don't be a fool, David, you don't know what it's like."

"I'm not leaving him there."

"I'm not coming with you . . . I mean it."

David pushes Iorweth away, sending him pitching into the wall below the Arabs.

"Like I say, Iorweth," he says, opening the door, "suit yourself."

Iorweth pulls off his cape and lets it drop as he listens to David running down the stairs and through the unlit house. Hears the farmhouse door open, then close, moves to the window and stares out through the cold and glistening glass, but there is nothing to be seen.

Nature is mad as David runs among it, buffeted in the blackness like an insane scarecrow. Mad nature matches his madness, flashing sudden idiot smiles of lightning through which the rain falls in endless silver bars. Hedges twist and sway, gripping desperate with their roots into the bubbling, sliding soil. Belly laughs of thunder and the darkness thick, though sudden shapes come as his eyes become part of the night.

Trees shake themselves like sea-wet dogs and the constant wind comes howling in slabs, puncturing his lungs, giving no rest, making every leaf, every blade, each twig and stone dance to its howl. It's a storm from Hell and Diabolus rides the slabs of wind, putting holes in the night with his laughter and pulling and biting at David's legs as he begins the climb towards Craig Point.

Through the madness he climbs, feeling nothing. Only his body takes the beating, his mind is dry and numb with the fear of what's to be done. On he goes, instinct pushing him while the Devil trips, stitch cutting him in half beneath his flopping cape. Falling, stumbling on through the fields of childhood and the lovely later-on times, the fields where Jenny had run, her hair a wing in the wind.

Halo'd in rain he moves in the cleavage of the valley, where Jenny in her dress of cornflower blue had fallen down like ring-a-roses with Alun Rhys and kicked her feet in the air with happiness. Scrambles now down the side of Craig Point, tiny stones cascading away from his feet in a continuous and miniature avalanche. Down he goes, like in a dream, when impatience with natural order makes the time and distance between a thought and its realisation disappear.

At the foot he pauses, crouching, not hearing his breath growling out of his throat, or feeling his head sandpapered by the knife-edge of the wind, or knowing his hands are torn and bleeding and the blood diluting as it slides across the rainy surface of his skin. Crouches like an animal in a sort of distant agony as the night is hair-cracked again by a fizz of lightning and in the two-second illumination he sees the huddled shape.

He kneels beside the body of his father, calling out "Dad" over and over, as the agony comes in close to him. God, his hands hurt now and his head feels frozen out of shape as he beats on the body with his bloody hands and calls out "Dad" to nothing.

Picks up the wet and heavy body now, fireman lift on to his shoulder, stumbles, falls, gets, up, crying like a baby, a cry which becomes a high mad-house moan. Yard follows yard, his father seeming to grow heavier with each second, a gigantic weight pressing him into the earth. His cape flaps and cracks like a tent flap, his eyes are filled with rain, putting his vision through a bottle bottom. Unfamiliar rocks grow in an instant before him, unexpected bushes block his way, the madness of the night is changing the geography and giving direction no meaning.

How far has it been? One mile? Two? Or only a hundred yards . . . and anyway a hundred yards to where? Once more he falls, falls beyond counting now, gasps on his knees beside the broken doll of his father. Gasps and rises again, movement beyond meaning now, a mad ballet in a cauldron. Tears off his cape and the wind plucks it away into the blackness like a prize, while the probing rain explores and covers his body in a second.

Picks up his father again, feels the heart-breaking weight across his shoulders, tries to move forward but his legs have died and turned to stilts and his father slips from his shoulders like a sack of peat. David stands for a second as though shot then finally falls to his knees again as another crack of thunder breaks his head and rhyme and reason float away. Victim at last to the vulture rain it seems to beat at him with a new energy forcing him down on to his father. David feels the stinging rain like a thousand tacks being hammered at his head and hands, feels himself slide away from his father's body and lie full length in the exploding soil.

"Oh, God!" he cries, his words making new bubbles in the mud, "Oh, God help me!"

David sees his father's face, the endless scratches, the eyes open and watery, belonging to a fish, the nose broken and different, the mouth wide, catching the rain. A little while ago that mouth had said "I love you, David" in the blackness of the yard. The last words David would hear from him, the very last, and now that mouth is open and catching rain. David lies, staring at the mouth, minute after minute, until it moves, and laughs, and snowflakes melt on its teeth.

Hand in hand David and his Dad clown through the snow, making patterns with their happiness. The snowman with a carrot nose watches them as they hoot with glee, doing a daft and giggling dance, idiots close to nature.

Now Mr James falls on his back, his mouth open to swallow air and snowflakes melt on his teeth. The snowflake mouth is shouting "The best snowman in Wales, boy, we've made the best snowman in Wales." David stares at the snowflake mouth, and it softens and the snow becomes rain.

"God help me," he says again, and his voice is faint and far-away and hanging outside of himself. Then his eyes close and everything ends.

When next he opens his eyes he sees again the face of his father, a face grotesque in death, and the rain has stopped at last, and all around birds are twittering and screeching after their fear. From where he lies he notices the trees and rocks become more definite as the light of the sky grows around them. Lies like that, only his eyes moving, letting time pass, the countryside grow clearer. Tries to move, but though the messages travel to the limbs they are ignored, the limbs have become part of the earth, the earth into which they press without feeling. David lets his eyes close again, feels near to death himself, and doesn't care. Nice it is to drift, in the dark of his head, to drift away, only the birds keeping him conscious.

No good though, the pain comes back, the pain and cold, beginning in his legs then filling his whole body, making him twitch and jerk like a fish out of water. Opens his eyes on the day growing brighter by the second, staggers, mud-covered and ungainly to his feet, sways, almost falls, spreads his legs wide, like a drunk, for balance.

Feels anger bubbling up in him now, anger at his impotence, at everything. Lunges forward at his father, grabs him by the collar, hauls him first to a kneeling position, then somehow upright. Drops him across his shoulders again, feels the weight again, and the lolling head beside his own.

Got to move now . . . *now* . . . one step, two, mud sucking at his feet, keep moving, make for that path, slipping, keep moving, no good, weakness, too weak, no good, keep moving, no good, no good. Left foot, right foot, walking through the pain, another step, one more, where's the path? One more step . . . one more . . . He reaches the path but feels his chest explode, and though he forces his stick-stiff legs to keep moving he knows now he'll never make it, never. Keeps moving though, staggering, stumbling.

"Help me!" he cries out as the chorus of birds grows louder. "Help me! Help me!"

Yard by yard he moves, legs beyond feeling, into the valley where the first rays of sun pierce the branches.

"Help me! Help me!!"

Then he falls, lies spreadeagled, gasping, defeated, hears himself begin to cry, and the little-boy tears roll down his face. Then his name is called.

"David!?"

The voice calls over to the right, sudden, unexpected, like a stab.

"David!?"

Iorweth's voice . . . Iorweth? Desperately David tries to rise, can't manage it, struggles with his idiot limbs.

"David, where are you?"

"Here . . . I'm here."

"David? . . . I can't see you, I can't see you."

"I'm here," screams David, lying immobile beside his father, "I'm here, I'm here, I'm here, I'm here."

Iorweth runs up and from David's angle looks vast against the sky. The face gaunt with fatigue, the eyes more opaque than ever, the reddish hair of him smeared against the forehead. Stands above them now, fighting for breath and words.

"I don't know why I came," he says, "I was just going to leave you, that's what I should have done, should have left you."

"Iorweth . . . help me."

"I told you not to try to carry him . . . I told you. I've had to leave Mam sleeping alone in the house. I told you the storm was too strong."

David moves like a crab, on his knees. "Please, Iorweth," he begs, "please."

Iorweth moves away towards a nearby tree, leans against the trunk of it, his hands in his pockets, his chin on his chest. Slowly David rises, stands for a moment, swaying, then moves with uncertain steps to Iorweth.

"We've got to get him home," he says.

Iorweth doesn't answer, just plucks a piece of the bark away and begins shredding it in the palm of his hand. David leans his right arm against the tree, puts his face in close to Iorweth.

"Please help me," he says.

93

Iorweth watches the bits of bark float away from his hand, dust the hand on his jacket. Then he moves away from the tree, moves slowly towards the body of Mr James, stands, legs apart, ten yards from it, studying it with a strange but cold interest.

David, leaning against the tree, feels the day still growing around them, an insane day, unreal, a joke. Surely in a moment Dad will get up, stretch himself, smile a bit foolishly and things will be as they were.

"All right, David," says Iorweth, "come on then."

So the unreal day is real enough and David walks from the tree and stands beside Iorweth and they bend over the body, Iorweth taking the shoulders, David the legs. Off they move, awkward, Mr James swinging loose and heavy and unhelpful between them like a hammock. David stumbles and falls, Iorweth watches, waits with indifference until David rises, lifts his father's legs, and they begin again the slow and painful journey to the farm.

In her bedroom, Mrs James sleeps fitfully. Her night has been broken by the storm and earlier by the sounds of David and Iorweth talking and shouting. In this strange, disturbed night she has drifted and dreamed. Dreams now, just below the surface.

Walks hand in hand with Robert, walks beside a stream, a stream turned into a sheet of glare by the sun. Feels love for Robert, does Alice, but knows it dies between them, her hand in his burnt by the ice-cold feel of it. Ahead, on the stream's edge, a young girl dressed in dazzling white almost becomes part of the water's iridescence as she pirouettes slow like something from a ballet. Robert stares transfixed at her, calls out "Mary", moves towards her, but she melts into the stream leaving only specks of light behind.

Specks of light which fall inside a bedroom, fall in time to the beating heart of Mrs James as she sees the bedroom door open and Robert standing there. A differ-

94

ent Robert, a Robert with smiling eyes and outstretched arms, arms which take her and lower her to the bed. Lips kiss her neck, hands stroke her breasts, hears herself cry "Robert". Feels the heavy breathing of him on her face, waits to hear him murmur her name but all he says is "Mary . . . Mary . . ." over and over.

She turns corpse cold beneath him, bites at the lips that said the name of Mary, pulls viciously at his hair, sees the hair straining at the roots, sees it turn to red, sees Robert's face change, age, thicken, coarsen, sees a red beard form, hears a crowded inn beneath them burst into song. Gives in to the stranger's drunken lovemaking, feels him thrusting deep inside her as the far-away singing gets louder. Feels the child growing inside her, moving, kicking, tries to hold it steady with her hands, but from inside her the baby cries out "Mam". Blackness now, then the child calls out again, the pitch different and close in her ear.

"Mam . . . Mam, wake up, it's me . . . Iorweth . . . wake up." Mrs James part opens her eyes and through the lines and blur of sleep sees Iorweth dark but outlined kneeling beside her bed. Smiles a little smile now and reaches out her arm to his shoulder.

"Oh . . . it's you, Iorweth . . . Oh! I was having such a dream . . ."

"Mam, listen . . ."

"Why have you woken me, Iorweth? What time is it?"

"It's nearly seven. Mam, listen . . ."

"Nearly seven?" says Mrs James, amazed, beginning to sense the mood of Iorweth.

"I've been out . . . with David, out by Craig Point."

"What?" says Mrs James, sitting up in bed, awake now, proper.

"Dad had an accident there . . . when he was mending the fences . . . slipped or something, I suppose . . . fell down Craig Point. David and me have been out . . . we've brought him back . . . he's dead, Mam."

95

"What?" says Mrs James again, her eyes staring in a world of seeming nonsense.

"He's dead, Mam."

Grabs him now, does Mrs James, grabs him by the shoulders and the strength of her makes him grunt.

"What are you saying?" she cries out, "what are you saying?"

"We brought him back," says Iorweth, wriggling in the grip. "He's downstairs . . . with David."

"Help me," she calls out, pulling at the sheets and blankets as though they were suddenly monsters pinning her to the bed, holding her in a nightmare. "Help me up. Oh God, help me up. I've got to go to him."

Iorweth joins the monsters though and holds her down.

"No, Mam . . . no."

"I've got to go to him . . . got to."

"Don't go, Mam, don't, he's not a sight to see."

"Iorweth . . ."

"He's not a sight to see."

Then suddenly Iorweth feels the strength go from her, watches in horror as her mind breaks into bits and a loud and terrible cry comes from her lips. A cry like he's never heard before, belonging to someone else. Takes her hands, quickly, tightly, hanging on desperately to something he feels is going.

"Mam . . . Mam, what is it?" he calls out, not understanding her strange agony at the death of someone she hated. "Mam, don't . . . don't cry like that."

The cry goes on, though, louder, like an animal or someone in Hell, as Iorweth releases her hands and kneels in pain and fear beside her bed shouting out—

"Don't . . . stop it Mam . . . stop it . . . don't, please don't . . . please don't . . . please don't . . ."

FIFTEEN

Sunshine has filled the days since the death of Mr James and today is no exception. Alun Rhys sits on a low stone wall a mile or so from the James' farm, kicks his heels against the stone and looks about him. The day is bright indeed, sharp and clear, with almost too much clarity. The edges of everything seem too defined, no matter how far away, and all the sounds are penetrating, seeming to disregard distance.

Alun, though, neither hears nor sees anything clearly, time has lost real meaning for him and become something to be filled until a moment comes to change the course of things. He's become now a stranger in his own home, a ghost, his father regarding him much as he regards the wallpaper or the stuffed birds in the parlour who stare through the years with false, button eyes.

His mother moves about him in an ache of embarrassment, pretending things are different, as she always does, as she always has, and even sister Annie, who talks to him the most, is drifting away and starting to live more and more in her own pretence.

Alun spends his free time coming to near the James' farm and just looking at it, hour after hour sometimes, not really knowing why, but unable to avoid it, unable to escape Jenny's ghost still pulling him there. So he sits on the wall in the sunshine, drumming his heels on the stones that have seen everything, drums his heels and waits like a traveller at a long-closed station, a traveller who dreams a train may come.

The sun is warm to his skin and washes him lovely, slowing him to stillness, till his legs hang unmoving and he sees only the road that leads to the farm.

Becomes so still he floats outside his body, looks down at it, sees it sitting all sad and still, feels Jenny about him, alive again, everyone alive, then feels only laughter for the silliness of things. The moment of peace passes and he is back again. Slowly beating his heels and staring at the road, seeing bits of glass float in the light and midges dart and swerve, changing their minds a dozen times within a foot.

To his left the road curves away out of sight and a mile down the road David walks towards the farm. Walks slow and thoughtful, letting the sun bathe him, wishing it would warm away the cold left by his visit to Annie only an hour ago. Behind him he hears the cloping of hooves, sharp in the clear air, sending birds hopping the hedge tops. Stops, turns, sees Daniel approaching. A wave of light brown dust washes over the horse's feet and breaks and spills among the wooden spokes of the cart wheels as Daniel jerks the reins and stops.

"Morning, Master David," he says.

"Morning, Daniel."

"Been to the village?"

"That's right. I've been to see Annie Rhys."

"Oh," says Daniel, lowering his head to his chest, letting the reins play through his fingers, his day spoilt.

"I wasn't very welcome," David goes on, coming in closer to the cart and resting his weight on one of the wheels. "She just stands around like something dead telling me I shouldn't go there. Don't know why I do, really. What are you going to say, Daniel? Let sleeping dogs lie?"

"Something like that," says Daniel, for that indeed was his thought. David runs his hand over the iron rim of the wheel, feels the heat of it on his finger-tips, watches them turn brown with the dust.

"Jenny didn't exist, did she?" he says, studying his fingers, then wiping them on his jacket. "Nothing happened, did it? Everything's fine . . . a sea of closed mouths. When I walk into the Rhys's home there's an air like ice and cold blank stares. When I came home from London Dad chattered around the subject . . . now Dad's dead too, and everything's fine."

David pauses, watches Daniel for a moment as though he might reply but Daniel only toys with the reins and then wipes his mouth with the back of his hand.

"Can I give you a lift back to the farm?"

"All right," replies David. "Thank you."

David pulls himself up into the cart which sways and creaks under the sudden movement and Daniel, glad of action, clicks his teeth, snaps the reins and moves the cart on. Peaceful it is jogging along in the sun and David closes his eyes and lifts his face up to it, feels it warm and friendly on his skin, sees it red at the back of his eyes.

"By the way, Daniel," he says, his eyes still closed, "I haven't really thanked you for coming to Dad's funeral."

"Oh, it was the least I could do," says Daniel. "He was a good man, your father, a good man."

They ride in silence for a while, listening to the steady beat of the hooves, just as they'd done that day when Daniel had brought him from the station and there had been so much to say that neither of them could really talk. Daniel, though, finally breaks the silence and says

"How's your mother, now?"

"Sickly," replies David, opening his eyes and watching tadpoles swim in the liquid countryside. "She just lies in her room day after day, never getting up, never going out. Just lies there, she does, with Iorweth sitting beside her, reading to her, hour after hour."

"And what does the doctor say?"

"He says she'll get over it . . . that's what he says."

A bird flies across their path, so close that Daniel has

99

to jerk back his head to avoid it. He watches it swoop just inches above a hedge, dart between the bars of a field gate which is held from dying by a piece of rope, then climb suddenly into the scalp of a tree.

"Well, anyway," says Daniel with a little laugh, "we've got a nice day for a change, birds singing, nice bit of sun, thank God for small mercies."

Thank God for small mercies indeed, but indeed they're small and David, though he welcomes the sun's warmth and the hum and buzz of the land about him and the gentle, jogging cart and the hooves kicking dust explosions in the road to home, can't rest in it.

"Daniel," he says, "do *you* think my father slipped on Craig Point?"

"What do you mean?" asks Daniel, clouds of puzzlement scudding his face.

"I mean do you think he slipped?"

"I don't understand."

"Doesn't matter," says David. "Only doesn't it seem strange to you that my father slipped? I mean he knew Craig Point like the back of his hand."

"What are you suggesting, Master David?"

"I just think it's strange, that's all," David says, sitting stiff and staring down at the horse's back where flies hover happy in the smell of meat.

"No good can come of prying, Master David."

"What are you afraid of, Daniel?" The question is flat and thrown-away.

"I'm not afraid of anything. I just think there's been enough sorrow . . . and you can only bring more through dabbling."

"I'm not *dabbling*." David is stung by the word, "I'm trying to find some *reason*. Reason for what happened to Jenny and what happened to Dad."

"No good can come of it," says Daniel, and David, seeing the walls go up gives a little laugh of hopelessness and says:

"No, of course not . . . everything's fine." So, on clops the horse who knows nothing of wonder or Welshness, while David and Daniel sit still and remote and the countryside about them stretches in the sun and watches and waits.

"Master David," says Daniel, sudden. "Over there, on that stone wall . . . it's the Rhys boy."

"Well, well, well," says David, his voice strange with surprise. "Stop the cart."

"Leave him be."

David stands up, staggers in the swaying cart and holds on to Daniel's shoulder for support. Cups his hands to his mouth now and calls out:

"I've just been round to your place. You never seem to be in these days. Why won't you talk?'

Daniel grabs his hand, holds it firm and says, "No point in all this."

David pulls himself free and shouts at the passive sitting figure.

"What are you doing this way? Why don't you answer? Why don't you answer? Stop the cart, Daniel."

"Master David . . ."

"Stop the cart!!"

Daniel pulls on the reins and the cart creaks and slithers to a halt as David leaps out over the dusty wheel. Daniel follows him, grunting with stiffness and dislike of it all. Follows him along the path, through a gap in the hedge that plucks at his hair and up the grass bank that leads to the wall. David jumps to the top of the wall, stands with his legs apart looking about him like a sailor seeking land, waits till Daniel joins him, gasping.

"He's gone," says David.

"Aye," says Daniel, "slipped away into those trees over there."

David crouches on his haunches, looks down at Daniel, sees sweat beads along the lines of the old forehead, then swings his legs over and sits on the wall as Alun had sat. Daniel leans against the wall, wipes away the beads with his coat sleeve and undoes the top button of his shirt. David sees the sweat glistening in the folds of Daniel's neck, sees the tufts of hair sprouting up from

101

above the desert of his vest, then picks up a small stone from the top of the wall and flings it away to where it falls in silence.

"God, Daniel," he says at last, "he does look like me . . . he does."

"Looks like you?" queries Daniel, his eyes closed, his face turning to water and running down his shirt. "What do you mean?"

"That's why Jenny let him . . . you know . . . that's why."

"Oh."

"He didn't have to run away . . . I only wanted to talk."

David flicks another stone away and it, too, lands in silence.

"Best we go back now," says Daniel. "Eh?"

"All right," says David, sliding from the wall and brushing the grey dust from his seat with his palms. "I wonder why he was here though."

They scuff together through the grass, wobbling like drunks down the bank and through the hedge hole.

"Funny, isn't it, Daniel," says David as they walk slow towards the horse and cart. "I'm at his place and he's at mine . . . why? Jenny dead, Dad dead . . . why? Mam sick and Iorweth reading away the hours to her. I'm not welcome at home, I'm not wanted at the Rhys's . . . So why do I go there? . . . Why?"

"Such a lot of questions, Master David."

"And the answers, Daniel?"

"No answers," says Daniel, clambering up into the cart and glad to feel the reins again.

"No answers," says David, pulling himself up and sitting beside him, "no answers . . . everything's fine."

Gently Daniel snaps the reins and the horse, whose life is just stop, wait and start, somewhere to somewhere, moves forward along the road to the farm, clopping steady under an umbrella of flies.

SIXTEEN

Summer has comfortably settled itself at last. Rivers and streams lap their way through the green and brown land to the sea. The farm unfolds itself, the wood of the barn expanding and deepening its cracks, the plaster between the stones of the house loosening and letting the stones stretch themselves in the burning heat.

Sometimes a warm and gentle breeze arrives from somewhere, noses its way around the farm, making the white lace curtains dance back against the plant on the sill, then fusses among the trees in the orchard before tiring of the heavy laziness of everything and pulling itself away over the fields and up beyond the stone glare of the mountains, to the place where winter waits.

In the orchard the sun drops through the gaps in the foliage and lands in dead many-shaped patches at the roots of the trees, while from one of the branches a broken swing hangs limp, useless and unwanted. Not far from the swing and in a pool of sun sits Mrs James in a wicker chair, her left hand resting on a gnarled brown walking stick, her right hand hanging over the chair arm, and looking something like the broken swing. Iorweth sits at the feet of her and with a small knife slowly shreds a twig to bits.

"What a lovely day, Iorweth," says Mrs James, her pale face made whiter by the light, "a lovely day, so still, I could sit here for ever. For ever, Iorweth, just you and me."

Iorweth brushes away some splinters of wood from his shirt front and smiles at her.

"Yes," he says, "but you mustn't stay out too long, now, you know what the doctor said."

"Oh, fiddlesticks to the old doctor. On a day like this I feel quite my old self again. Doesn't everywhere look lovely in the sun?" She closes her eyes and remembers other sunny times, different times and feels a sadness for it. Iorweth rises and goes over to the swing, pushes it with his foot and watches it drift backwards and forwards, the wooden seat weatherbeaten and breaking up, hanging from only one rope support. The other rope hooked like a snake on one of the branches dangles finished and frayed and ready to tear except at hand height where it seems oiled and stiff. Leaves glide down in the swing's sudden movement and Iorweth catches one and slowly splits it along its veins.

"I'm going to miss this farm when we leave," he says.

"Me too, lovey . . . me too."

The swing's wooden seat bangs against the bark of the tree, shudders, spins and stops. Iorweth turns and comes back to the wicker chair, lies on his back beside it and looks up at the sky between the trees. Hears now the distant bleat of sheep, the nearby hum of bees and the warmth of the earth on his back. Mrs James looks down at him, like a dog at her feet, he is, and she feels happy in the moment and rests inside herself.

"When is David leaving us?" asks Iorweth, seeming not to move a muscle of his body.

"Should be soon now."

"He keeps hanging on . . . first for Jenny, then for Dad . . . just hanging on."

"It won't be long."

Iorweth comes to life sudden and crouches intense at his mother's feet.

"I want us to be together," he says, his eyes strange, bright, his hand reaching out and lying softly moving in her lap, "just you and me, Mam, like it should be."

"We'll be together," she says.

"I want to look after you, take care of you, make you well again. When David goes there'll be just you and me . . . like we used to talk about in the bedroom at night . . . whispering and hugging."

"Those talks," says Mrs James, smiling, fond, "those long talks and you with your eyes on fire."

"It's all coming true . . . nothing can change it."

"I hear there's talk of war," Mrs James says, unexpected.

"War?"

"Only rumours, of course . . . the doctor was saying . . . only rumours."

Iorweth gets up and moves away a bit, fear churning him about.

"I won't go," he says, his voice trembling with uncertainty and things going sudden wrong, "I won't go . . . I won't leave you."

"Give me your hand, Iorweth," says Mrs James, and she takes it as he comes in close to her, links the fingers in a firm, sure grip that's supposed to tell of comfort but he feels only the strange, unnatural cold of her hand.

"David can go," says Iorweth, "*he* can go."

"Do you hate him very much?"

"Of course I do," Iorweth says, his voice rising in uncertainty and doubt of everything and pulling back his hand from the bloodless grip. "Of course I do . . . why do you ask? . . . I hate him like you do."

"It's funny, Iorweth, but there's no hate any more." She pauses for a second as though listening with interest to what she's saying, then goes on, "After all this time . . . no hate."

Things are falling apart for Iorweth, things which seemed certain are turning traitors.

"Mam!" he cries.

"There's no love either . . . just nothing. Silly old life but I can't rub it out, and now I'm old before my time and filled with sickness."

"You'll get better, Mam, I promise . . . I promise."

"The point is, Iorweth," she says, suddenly leaning forward and taking his hand again, "try not to hate too much. I know it's my fault, but I'm asking you to try to stop now."

"Sinners must be punished," Iorweth shouts, trying to pull his hand away, but she holds it with unexpected strength.

"We're all punished, boy," she says, "all of us. I wanted to hurt everybody, *everybody*, but in the end I've hurt myself most of all."

"Stop it, Mam, stop it now." He breaks free from her grip and walks away back to the broken swing where he just stands in stillness, staring at it. Slowly, and with considerable effort, Mrs James rises from her chair, stands for a moment gathering strength, while the pool of sunlight shrinks around her, then, leaning heavily on her stick, comes to behind Iorweth.

"It's getting dark, Iorweth," she says. "Nice days don't last."

He wants to cry, does Iorweth, cry like a baby, all tears and sobs. Wants to hug his Mam, hug her hard, and kiss and cry, but he keeps his back to her until she touches it with her hand and he turns and says:

"Come on, Mam. I'll help you indoors."

So together they walk from the orchard, leaving behind the wicker chair and the swing and the day, and the sun which watches them go turns the rails red ahead of Alun's train. Smoke drifts past the carriage where Alun sits alone in the corner seat, drifts past the window and lies on the hedges. Alun watches Wales grow redder and darker, watches it moving away from him, perhaps for ever.

Remembers his father standing behind him as he had packed, no words, a ceremony only. Alun closes the suitcase and, without even looking at each other, he and his father leave the bedroom. Mr Rhys closes the bedroom door, then takes a key from his waistcoat pocket and the door is locked as though sealing up sickness. Down the creaking stairs and past the open living-room door, where inside sits Mrs Rhys, staring at her hands on her lap and plucking at her dress like Annie. Annie herself has gone walking in the devil's dip beyond the bridge, unable to say goodbye.

"Well, Mam, I'm off then," says Alun.

There's no reply, though, just silence and plucking her dress and a father who's walked down the hall and opened the front door.

Down the hill from the house he goes, past the children bubbling as they run in circles, past the chapel, where later his parents will kneel and challenge God to tell them they've done wrong. Over the bridge, where for a moment he thinks he sees Annie in the trees by the dip, but whoever it is is soon lost to sight. The case grows heavier, pulling him into the soil, but he moves on quicker and soon it's the station and the train.

So, perhaps for ever, Wales moves away from him past the carriage window, and Alun puts his face in close to the glass, feels the cool of it. Away it goes, redder and darker, till soon all he can see is his own sad reflection staring back at him.

Stares back at him, too, from the shop windows of London, where now in the first days of August the city and its people are caught in the excitement of possible war.

Through the streets he walks, as David had walked on his arrival, but it's a different London from the one David had first encountered, it's playing a different tune. Germany has invaded Russia and the Grand Duchy of Luxemburg, and the gravity of the international position is fully comprehended in London. Though, true to say, that in the streets and hotels and theatres, in fact wherever people are gathered, the talk is of war, there is no suggestion of shrinking from the issues. Nobody wants war, but no one will shrink from it if the occasion demands it.

Except, that is, for Mr George Senway, the owner of

14 Elm Drive, a shabby but respectable house where Alun has been given lodgings. Five feet six of fading fire is Mr Senway, disappearing weakly into the caverns of his ash-stained clothing. The eyes, though, are bright and alive as he looks at Alun and says

"We find ourselves, young man, in what may prove to be the greatest conflict in the whole history of Man, the whole history." He sips his herb tea from a blue china cup and continues. "The conditions, though, that have made this situation possible are completely non-Christian . . . *completely*. No country, no church, indeed no individual can escape the blame."

He rises from the clinging comfort of the brown velvet-covered chair and crosses to the window. Stares out across the lines of washing and flowers growing sad in squads to the distant park where a little girl, all pink and golden, jumps up and down by herself.

"If we're going to deal out blame," goes on Mr Senway, "then let us not fail to blame ourselves first."

Alun listens, not really understanding, just watches the ailing old man standing in the window's light, wonders about him and about the life he has had. The old man turns from the window and places his teacup upon the oak fire surround.

"And may God forgive us," he says, "may Almighty God forgive us."

The fourth of August comes now and Alun does nothing but walk the streets, walks among the seething, excited crowds, feels that excitement in his veins, sees at last some purpose for himself. The crowds grow and grow, extending from Trafalgar Square to the House of Commons, where the greatest number gather about Downing Street.

Alun, feeling less like a stranger than he's ever felt in his life, becomes part of the cheering, flag-waving throng, waits for the wave that will wash him somewhere. Taxi-cabs carve their way through the crowds, taxi-cabs filled with young men singing the 'Marseillaise', and as evening gathers the whole of London, it seems, waits for the receipt of Germany's reply to Britain's ultimatum.

Stands among it, does Alun, feeling protected by being part of its intensity, stands among it and watches as the people cheer each and every minister. Then the news of the Declaration of War and the greatest cheer of all, a roar around London that sends the pigeons and sparrows fluttering about the night.

Alun is pushed and jostled and carried along now, eyes are filled with tears and strangers shake hands. Trafalgar Square becomes impassable, the mad feel of mafficking is in the air, while in Soho and the foreign quarters of London Germans and French, their bags packed, make ready for instant departure.

Alun stumbles through the madness of the night, feeding on the excitement, dances wildly with a fat woman in Charing Cross, and only in the occasional lull does he think of Mr Senway and the thin, sad lips of him saying "God forgive us!"

Hardly sleeps at all, does Alun, a few hours only of restless tossing and turning, the decision though is made, his course is set and as day spills over his bed he rises eagerly to face it. Dresses quickly and leaves the house and the sleeping Mr Senway, who snores now in the bedroom filled with the bric-a-brac of another time, a time that's over for everyone. Laughs and cheers with the crowds, joins the masses of young men who now surge around the recruiting stands in Horse Guards Parade. Pushes his way through and shouts out his name to the Recruiting Sergeant, shouts it out loud for the world to hear.

Walks on air now, feels a friend of everyone, happy in the martial mood of a city that's all bands and cheering and flags. Walks link-armed with another half-dozen young men who have sworn themselves to Kitchener, and they roar and yell like fighting bulls and whistle with bravado at the pretty girls.

Night comes, and in the public house humanity seethes like grubs in an angler's tin, thick smoke softens the edges of everything, people cough holes in the air as beer spills from table tops. Everyone is shouting and laughing, patriotic songs burst spasmodically from smoke-hidden corners. There's an excess of back-slapping and bottom-patting and calling for more drinks.

By the door, beneath a picture of John L. Sullivan, sits a prostitute, her eyes sharp and sober. Her over-red mouth sips at the glass, leaving a smear. Slowly she sips, and waits. Alun, stupid with drink, spills some of it down his shirt and laughs. God! The world is going round, colours and smoke and singing, everything moving, moving in noise so that nothing matters. Pulls his tie loose as the heat pushes the sweat from him. Takes off his collar and shoves it with his tie into his pocket. Giggles as another drink is shoved into his hand, giggles and watches women laughing too loud with wide-open mouths and men hugging each other in sudden maudlin friendship. Gulps at his drink and giggles again as more flows down his front. Scrambles sudden now on to a table top as his friends clap daft at him. Stands there, he does, with his beer slopping out of his glass, extends his free hand and yells above the noise:

"Your King and country need you."

Those who notice him give a cheer and some mock salutes.

"If every patriotic young man answers her call," Alun shouts on, having memorised the posters word for word, "then England and her Empire will emerge stronger and more united than ever."

A great cheer now, and as Alun raises his slopping pint above his head in acknowledgment of the ovation his foot skids on the beery surface of the marble table top and he crashes unceremonious to the floor. Lies among the beer and fags, he does, listening to the screams of far-away laughter, feeling everything spin and dip. Lies feeling magnetised to the floor as the place becomes a mad roundabout of chair legs, trousers, skirts and lights like stars.

Feels a sudden warmth spread along his left thigh, hears a voice yell out "Look . . . Taffy's pee'd himself."

Laughter and shouting and embarrassed squeaks from the ladies as he is hauled to his feet.

"They won't stand for that in the army," shouts another voice as Alun pushes away the hands and stumbles towards the door.

"You can come with me, Taffy dear," says the prostitute, rising like a mechanical doll. "I'll see you all right."

"Go to hell," shouts Alun, fumbling for the door handle on the wrong side, then finds it, pulls it open and steps outside to loud and long cheers.

SEVENTEEN

Outside the pub he leans, slack and ill, against a rusting rain-spout, feels a breeze bringing welcome cool and blowing empty cardboard boxes down the street. In his spinning head Alun hears a voice say,

"You feeling all right, chum?"

His eyes focus on a young man standing beside him, a man he remembers from inside the pub, a man who has stood in the corner all night drinking quietly and alone.

"Yes, I'm all right," replies Alun, feeling removed from everything and aware of the sick in the pit of his stomach. "Just leave me alone."

"Do you want to be sick?" asks the man.

"Just shut up."

"Where do you live then?"

"Nowhere . . . leave me alone."

Alun hears himself speaking as though from a great distance. Everything is too much effort, talking, thinking. Feels now his back sliding down the wall, realises he's sitting stupid on the pavement, remembers for a moment that his collar and tie are in his jacket pocket, smells the beer on his clothing, feels the damp urine on his trouser leg cool. Then the sick comes out of him, freely, without effort, spewing on to the pavement, sees his hand in it, feels the blackness close around him, then silence.

Sounds in his head of shuffling feet and the realisation that his arm is around the man, and that they are weaving along together somewhere, and the man is saying "Steady now, won't be long." Alun allows himself to be half-carried, half-dragged through the streets as they walk away from Bow Bridge and out towards Stratford East. Gas lamps light their stumbling way. "You'll be all right, that's it, you'll be all right."

A horse-drawn cab clops lonely on its way back to the city but they let it pass and weave on, with each step for Alun bringing him, it seems, from the point of death. Then a pause as Alun heaves noisily against a wall, but nothing comes up, just sound, and the man waits a yard or two away and lights a cigarette. A tram then comes at them out of the night, dimly lit and clanging loud it sways towards them, its single beam headlamp a searchlight in the gloom.

"Come on," coaxes the friend, grabbing Alun by the arm and pulling him along the street like a rag doll. God! Dying would be lovely, but there's only running and stumbling and the tram jolting behind them. The tram driver on his exterior platform sees them running wildly along the pavement, reaches out his large gloved hands and winds desperately now at the big, brass handle. Alun sees it stop behind them, a hiss of steam and a jarring of wheels. A deep maroon and cream monster it is, and his friend pulls him aboard and slumps breathlessly beside him in the corner seat as the tram starts up again and buildings flash by the windows.

Alun stares stupid at the window, feeling too bad to think, just letting things happen, everything out of his hands now. Stares in silence as houses go dimly past, a ghostly figure seen for a second in the glow of the yellow gas light, the conductor and his friend talking and laughing together . . . about him? And all the time the droning din of the electric motors.

Then the stop and Alun almost falls as he gets off but keeps his balance and stands swaying in God knows where. "Come on," says the man, "this way." The tram whines off into the night, its number stencil gleaming like a star, a star which Alun watches go, growing smaller till it goes out in the distance. They walk on for a while, another tram passes them, a tram filled with dockers, it clangs across a junction on its way to the river. Alun stops sudden now and smooths back his hair with his hands, feeling better and more sober. From his pocket he takes his collar and tie and puts them on while his friend watches, smiling.

"Where are we?" asks Alun.

"Stratford."

"What's happening then?"

"You passed out . . . you were in a bad way, so I decided to bring you back to my place . . . all right?"

"I suppose so . . . thanks anyway."

"Don't mention it. It's not far now."

"Good."

In the distance shunting engines in the Stratford yards chugg monotonous between the wagons as the man takes Alun's arm again.

"What's your name?"

"Alun . . . what's yours?"

"Michael . . . Mike."

So Alun and Mike walk on, smiling a bit foolishly at each other, feeling daft in the dark, until they reach the terraced house where Mike lives. Very much a working-class house this, nothing but essentials, and the objects in it seem to droop with lack of love. Everything clean, mind you, but looking bored.

"Sit there, Alun," says Mike, lowering him gently on to a sofa, "I'll make some tea." Alun, though, stops him with a question.

"Where's your parents?"

"Oh, they live about a mile away."

"You live here by yourself, then?"

"That's right," says Mike, sitting on the arm of the sofa, an arm that's shining from hundreds of sittings, "I was married, as a matter of fact, for just over eight years then she upped and left me. Bloody cheek, really.

Still . . . good riddance." He gives a little laugh, not very convincing.

"I'm sorry," says Alun, feeling ridiculous and wishing to God he'd never gone into the pub.

"Not to worry," says Mike, "I've got myself a nice, new little girl friend, comes round most nights. She may be along later, as a matter of fact, she's at a meeting."

"Meeting?"

"A B.S.P. meeting." Alun just stares so Mike goes on, "British Socialist Party."

"Oh, you're a socialist, then?"

"Well, of course . . . aren't you?"

"I don't know what I am, I don't think about politics much."

"Well, you should do. I mean, a Welshman like yourself. Look at the terrible deal Wales has had. What about Tonypandy then?"

"Well . . ."

"What's more, are you sure you're joining the army?"

"Of course I'm sure."

"You're a fool . . . do you know that?"

"Fool? . . . Why?"

"It's a long story, Alun . . . but it's not our war."

"What are you talking about," says Alun, feeling more sober by the second. "Of course it's our war. Whose war is it then?"

"The money-makers, chum, the capitalists, it's their bloody war. Honest, when I saw all you blokes in the pub tonight, all of you so happy to be going to war it made me feel ill. You don't know what it's *about*."

"I just think that it's our patriotic duty to . . ."

"Patriotic duty? It's not patriotism, it's *profit*, that's what it is, profit."

Alun feels the props knocked away from under him, there's no peace anywhere. For a while his escape from Wales and the prospect of army service in the defence of King and Country had seemed like a patch on his pain, but now it's all being destroyed. Up gets Mike, unable to sit, moves about the loveless room while Alun sits looking at his feet and the empty fireplace and the little wooden clock above it that creeps along the mantelpiece with the vibrations of Mike's footsteps.

"Profit," goes on Michael, "not patriotism. The only sort of patriotism we should have is *class* patriotism. Why the hell should we kill each other just for the capitalists? Let the British capitalists and the German capitalists sort it out among themselves. Why should we do their dirty work for them? What have they ever done for us? What? I mean . . . look at me. I work at the Stratford railway yards, work myself to death, and what for? For a house like this? And there's plenty worse off than me, my parents for example. We're not only *born* working class, chum, we're *kept* working class. And now those that have seen to it that we're kept this way want us to have our bloody brains shot out for them. Well, let *them* go out and defend their ruddy property, let *them* all blow each other to hell, and when they've gone perhaps we'll really have something to defend."

"Sure, sure," says Alun, not really knowing what to say.

"There's going to be a revolution in this country one of these days. When the people wake up, when people like you wake up and realise that you spend the whole of your lives running around in a treadmill and touching your forelock every time you get patted on the head."

"Is that why you brought me here? To give me all this stuff?"

"No, of course not. I just felt sorry for you, that's all."

"Well, don't. Anyway, I've got a headache."

"I'm sorry," says Mike, moving to the mantelpiece and putting the clock back on its original mark. "I'll make that tea."

He moves to the door which is covered in thick, treacly, brown gloss paint, opens it and goes out, leaving Alun staring into the fireplace at the ashes and old cigarette packets. The thumping in his head grows deeper and pain forms a band behind his eyes.

"Oh . . . hello!" says a surprised female voice behind him. He turns his head and the pain inside it slops about like water in a bucket. He sees a young lady standing by the door from the hall.

"Are you Michael's girl friend?" he asks.

"Is that what he called me?"

"I got drunk tonight. He brought me here."

"Fine." She comes into the room and begins to unbutton her long, dark green coat. "Where is he now?"

"Making some tea." Alun watches her. A fine face she's got, intelligent, moves well too, with all the confidence in the world.

"Good," she says, and then, "you're a Taffy, are you?"

Alun feels the word sting him again, as it had done in the pub. Doesn't know why really, only knows it does.

"That's right," he says, anger making his words sudden hard. "I'm a Taffy and I'm going to join the army tomorrow and fight for the capitalists . . . what do you think of that?"

"Not much," she says, smiling gently.

"No, I don't suppose you do," says Alun, rising painfully to his feet, trying desperate to muster some dignity, and wishing to hell he didn't stink of sick and pee. "I don't suppose you do, you and your friends. But somebody's got to do the bloody fighting, somebody's got to and it might as well be bloody stupid Taffys like me."

"I don't think you're stupid," she says.

"Well, I *am*," replies Alun, crossing to the door, "I *am*, and that's the end of it."

"No, don't go . . . please stay."

"No, thank you," he says, opening the door, stepping back into the hall, and falling against a bicycle that's propped against the cream-painted dado. " I've had enough."

He has, too. He doesn't know what he thinks any more, about anything or anybody. He straightens the bicycle.

"What about the tea?" asks the girl.

"I don't want it. I'm going. I'll get home somehow."

He moves down the hallway, opens the front door, hears the night wind gathering strength, sees the gas lamps flickering down the road ahead.

"Thank Mike for the consideration and the conversation but tell him that Taffy's gone to war. Tell him I've gone because I don't care about the reasons and tell him that with a bit of luck one of these days he'll get his revolution and that with a bit of luck I'll get my bloody brains blown out."

He zigzags off down the road, giddy and lonely in the gas light. In the head of him he hears already the bark of commands that will bring an end to zigzag movement and bring order. The world is spinning but there's a change in things. Tonight has been as unreal as the ocean pavement on which he rides and the rubber gas lamps that bend under the tilting half-orange sky.

It's all been daft tonight, the drink and the pee, and the tram with its searchlight eye, and capitalists fighting capitalists, all daft. There's a change. No more Wales where days are born old at dawn, no more nibs scratching, no more clocks marking out nothing, no more offices in Wales or here in London making records of someone for someone. There's a change, and the discipline starts now in the wobbly world as he steadies himself, holds his shoulders back smart, looks straight ahead beyond the Stratford railway yard and starts a sort of march into the darkness.

The girl watches him go, until not even the echo of his shoes is left. Stands there, hearing faint shunting sounds in the distance and remembering another time, another orange night, and another Welshman she left reading a letter, a letter that told of the death of his sister. Helen goes in, closing the door, leaving the night to itself.

118

EIGHTEEN

The farm, though, is untouched by London's fever. As in most places in the land where people are few and scattered, there is none of the excitement and anxiety of war. There is precious little news of things and little want of any.

The summer's day has darkened and chilled to evening and in the living-room Mrs James and Iorweth sit together in oil-light, much as they had done days earlier in the sun of the orchard. Her hands move slowly, methodically, the thin pale fingers pushing wool on to ebony needles from which a red jersey grows, the colour vivid against the black of her dress. The rocking chair creaks to her gentle movement and Iorweth listens to this sound that goes down the years, listens and watches with worry, worry that like a heap of dust she will suddenly blow away and there'll be nothing.

Watches, too, the world grow black outside the tiny window, a few shapes for a while then only black glass with lights in it, and as the world dies outside the room becomes more close, and not only a room but a place inside his head where happiness is. To go on forever like this, just him and Mam cocooned from troubles and seasons, just the two of them, that's all he could wish for.

"Soon have the jersey finished now, Iorweth," says Mrs James. "Then winter can come and blow all it likes." She knits in silence for a while then turns towards him and says, "Hold out your hands and help me wind some wool, lovie."

He crouches beside her chair and proffers his hands like a criminal for handcuffs. From a dark green carpet bag Mrs James pulls a fresh skein of wool and drapes it across the hands of him.

"I like red," he says, "red's a good colour."

"All colours are good," she replies, and somewhat oddly considering she hardly ever gets out of black. "All of them, all are good." As a thin snake of wool squirms away from his wrists and up into the growing red ball Mrs James holds in her hands, Iorweth leans forward and kisses the hands, bringing a pause to things.

"Well, now," she says, looking surprised and fond, "what was that for?"

"Just for love."

"They're not hands for kissing any more, Iorweth love, they're old and tired like me."

"They're lovely hands," Iorweth says, pressing his cheek against them, and feeling again the unexpected ice.

"Lovely indeed," she exclaims, "they're white and bony and lined with blue."

Iorweth snaps in sudden as his worry worms wriggle, "Don't talk of age."

"Age is with us . . . like the air."

"Don't talk of it."

Mrs James reaches out a hand and glides it across his hair. "Such a worry head," she says, "everything worries you."

"In a few months," says Iorweth, and his voice is harsh as though issuing orders, "we'll go for long walks."

"Yes, boy, if you say so."

"Long walks together."

"More likely you'll be pushing me in a wheelchair," laughs Mrs James, starting to wind in the thin red snake again.

"Long *walks*," shouts Iorweth, as though sound itself can banish age and illness, "we'll go walking and laughing and talking, honest, Mam."

"Well, don't forget, lovie, that we shan't be here at the farm, we'll have moved by then. There won't be long lanes and fields for walking."

"There'll be roads and streets," says Iorweth, who'd walk his mother through a barbed wire hell rather than let time take her from him and spoil his dream. "We'll have lovely walks, me in my red jersey, you in your hat." Makes her smile, does this, and he goes on. "Think of it, Mam, think of it—you and me—walking—every day—and soon you'll feel better, your legs will grow strong again and the white will go away from your face and you'll never be sickly again, not ever."

"Iorweth, love . . ." she says to stop him and bring calm, but Iorweth goes on.

"I don't want you to be like this, Mam, sitting and staring and sometimes strange."

"How, strange?"

"Like there's things in your head I can't hear and I don't like it."

"But I'm so much better," she says, sudden surprised at him.

"Yes, but I want it to be like it was—and it will be —when we move—when we go for our walks."

"We'll see, love, we'll see, when the time comes."

A pause, now, except for the slow winding of the wool and the long, sad squeak of the rocking chair. The oil lamp dims a bit, stretching their shadows and putting caves of black in the corners. Iorweth hears the ceiling groan above them. David is walking about in the bedroom, David who won't leave them.

"It'll seem funny not living on a farm," says Iorweth.

"Well, you can hardly call it a farm any more," Mrs James says, winding in the last of the wool and placing the ball in her lap, "with nearly all the animals sold out and everything."

"I wish I could keep the bees," says Iorweth, "I love the bees."

"There'll be no place for bees, Iorweth."

Rises now, does Iorweth, moves back to his chair in a

dark patch of the room, sits and stretches out his legs, sees his boot caps glint in the light.

"Remember that story you used to tell me?" he says, "years ago, about bees settling on the dead branch of a tree?"

"Good Lord," exclaims Mrs James in the memory of it, "I'd almost forgotten."

"You said there was a superstition in Wales that if a swarm of bees settled on the dead branch of a tree then death would come to the bee-keeper's family before winter."

"Yes, I remember."

"Well, shall I tell you something?" says Iorweth, leaning forward and not waiting for an answer. "Early in May I was standing by the burnt-out tree at the back of the orchard—and when I looked at that black branch —the one that looks like a hand—there was a swarm of bees on it." Mrs James fingers the ball of wool, hears the ceiling creak above her.

"I don't believe it," she says, "you're making it up."

"No, Mam," says Iorweth, slow, definite. "They were there."

"A head full of fancy."

"No, Mam, they were *there*, and it came true, didn't it . . . death came."

"That's quite enough, Iorweth."

"It came to Jenny, it came to Dad."

"I forbid you to say any more."

"It was *you* who told the story," says Iorweth, moving to Mrs James and shouting the words down at her. Angry at the slow change in her, he is, a change that's making her a stranger. Angry, he is, that she doesn't share his excitement at the bees and what they have brought.

"It's just a silly superstition, that's all," says Mrs James, "nothing to it at all."

"All the same," says Iorweth, putting his face a kiss away from hers, "I saw those bees . . . and I knew."

A sound to the left and turning Iorweth sees David

come in, a book under his arm. Sees him cross to the oil lamp and sit at the one-legged table that is covered in a yellow cloth of light. Sees him open the book, flick through the pages, a gooseberry . . . unwanted.

"Have you heard the story of the bees, David?" asks Iorweth.

"What story," says David, his eyes on the turning pages.

"The story that if a swarm of bees settle on a dead branch of a tree then death will come to the bee-keeper's family before the year is out."

"No, I haven't heard it." The page flicks. "Why?"

Iorweth brings a small chair to the opposite side of the table, sits in it the wrong way round, his arm resting on the back of it, his face in close to David, trying to pull his eyes up from the pages.

"Early this year," says Iorweth, "some of the bees swarmed on to that dead tree out at the back . . . and it came true, didn't it? . . . Death came . . . Strange, don't you think?"

"I think you're talking your usual rubbish."

"Jenny dead . . . Dad dead . . ."

Mrs James moves sudden in the rocking chair. "Iorweth!" she shouts, and the ball of wool rolls from her lap and makes a long, red vein across the floor. "I've forbidden you to speak any more of it."

"Only David remains," goes on Iorweth, remorseless. "Tell him to go, Mam."

"Now then, Iorweth," says Mrs James, her voice a warning note, but Iorweth is deaf to inflection. There's a door to be beaten down and nothing now will stop his battering.

"Tell him, Mam, tell him."

David slams shut his book with a bang that makes the ghosts shiver and wait for a tearing of things. Up jumps David, the chair falling backwards from him like a knocked-out boxer.

"Yes, Mam, tell me," says David, moving in to his mother and letting the wool gash across his legs. "Tell

123

me to go from you. Tell me to leave you alone with your Iorweth. Come on, tell me."

Mrs James begins to rock wildly in the chair as though it were a wooden horse that could somehow rock her away from here, from pain. "Leave me alone," she shouts, "both of you leave me alone."

"Not *me*," cries Iorweth, coming at her out of the shadows. "Not *me*, Mam, not now. All those dreams, you can't blow them away. I won't let you go. You belong to me."

Mrs James stops rocking and fixes him with eyes of stone. "Belong?" she questions, her voice strange. "Belong?"

David feels the tide running his way. "Tell him it's over, Mam," he says sudden, to catch the tide. "Tell him things have changed. Why don't you say it?"

"Nothing's changed," screams Iorweth, "nothing at all."

"He's fanning dead fires, Mam. Tell him to stop."

Mrs James rises, gasping, and moves like an injured crow away from her chair, which, free of its rider, gallops madly on the spot.

"Leave me be," she says, "I'm going to my room."

Iorweth moves quickly to her side, takes her arm, leans in close. "I'll come with you, Mam," he says. "I'll stroke your hair like always, I'll whisper to you like always. Nothing's changed."

"Leave me be," Mrs James says again, pulling her arm free, but Iorweth grabs it again, a drowning man and a straw.

"Nothing's changed, Mam, nothing," he cries, "I'll come with you, let me come with you. Nothing's changed."

"Iorweth, leave me be or by God I'll strike you."

For a moment he almost relaxes his grasp, then he holds her tighter, tighter, pressing his fingers through her arm, pushing himself into her body.

"I'll strike you, Iorweth."

"Mam!" he cries, in a despair of not being able to stop things.

Then her hand blurs white in the dimming light and stings across Iorweth's face. For a moment the face of him is shocked and dead, his opaque eyes staring out as though disbelief were pushing them from the back. The awful crack of flesh on flesh hangs in the air for seconds like a doom bell and Iorweth, moaning low like an animal, slips slowly to his knees. A silence now, as though all Wales has stopped, and only the distant pendulum tick of the hall clock shows that time is still going on. A fly from somewhere circles over Iorweth's bent and moaning head, then lands blackly on the back of his collar.

"Leave him be," says David quietly, "don't touch him, Mam, don't comfort him . . . it's over . . . it's over, Mam . . . leave him . . . leave him . . . leave him . . ."

Slowly Mrs James begins to reach out her hand towards the crumpled figure at her feet.

"Leave him," says David, louder now. "Leave him."

The hand retreats a little, stops, and suddenly the flood gates of emotion are opened and Mrs James holds Iorweth's head against her thighs and strokes and strokes the hair of him.

"I'm sorry, I'm sorry," she says. "Don't cry, don't cry, Iorweth, I didn't mean to hit you, didn't mean to. I didn't mean it, love, didn't mean . . . Don't cry, all over, all forgotten, don't cry now." Iorweth is moaning into her dress, his arm around her legs.

"Mam . . . Mam . . ."

David stands watching like a statue, and when he speaks his voice is dead. "Mam," he says, "you should have . . . you should have . . ." and he stops.

"There now," says Mrs James, still stroking and comforting, "all the pain will soon be gone . . . there now . . . Mam's sorry."

She stoops and kisses the top of Iorweth's head as David calls out "Don't kiss him." His words are like a bitter order. "Don't kiss him, Mam."

"Iorweth," croons Mrs James, all soothing, "Iorweth, baby."

David comes to her and their eyes meet, on guard.

"Did you see his face, Mam?" asks David, a kind of exultation about him now. "When you hit him . . . did you see his face? Did you see his face? . . . Did you see his face?"

He grabs his mother's head in his hands, holds it tight and cries out, "Did you? Did you?" over and over until she pulls his hands away. David bursts now into laughter, strange wild laughter, so wild indeed that even Iorweth looks up from the comfort of his mother's skirts and watches with wonder. On and on goes the mad laughing, pouring from David as though he is possessed, while Mrs James and Iorweth stand in the sound of it, ships in a storm. Slowly the laughter subsides and David leans for a moment against a chair back, letting the exultation drip away to stillness, before picking up his book and going upstairs.

NINETEEN

The following day is dying in a blazing sunset as David crosses the old stone bridge that stands in the middle of the village. Around him, rooftops are on fire with the evening, streaks of red splash down cottage walls and form pools in corners. Everywhere the stones are bleeding. Thin Welsh cats, halo'd in red and gold, yeowl across the fences and purple clouds grow by the second over the distant hills.

The streets are empty, the windows open, breathing deep, no sound, though, except for the river passing through, glad to be gone, and the muffled sound of hymns from the chapel. In the red and gold and quiet of everything time is not a passing thing and Wales for a while is gentle.

David sits on a wall opposite the chapel, a wall that's been warming its ancient heart all day, feels the heat of it pass through his trousers and into his legs, and in the spreading warmth and wash of hymns is lulled to nothing.

The creak of the chapel's iron gate pulls him back and standing there, dressed in Sunday black, is Annie. So pale her face, paler than ever, and smaller, too, it seems with no light in the eyes, no warmth in the lips, a face with the person gone, a photo face. Stands there, she does, all black and pale, framed by the large, grey gate supports, and the thinning sun through the iron bars puts stripes down her skirt.

She is part of the shadows, part of the stones. Like Mam at home, thinks David, Mam, rocking in her chair, her lined, bony hands resting on the chair arms and becoming part of the grain. Like Iorweth, who can kick away at a mound of autumn leaves and disappear. Welsh people don't live in places, they *are* the places, the people are the same as the sky and the marshes, the rivers and mountains and sea and rain, they're all made from the same stuff, and the fact that some of the stuff decides to take human shape, like the English and others, is just a huge Welsh joke. People who have managed to shut their ears to the deafening and misleading silence say that the whole of Wales is covered in the sound of laughter.

"Oh . . . it's you again," says Annie.

"Yes."

"There's nothing to say," she says and turns to walk up the hill. David slides down from the wall, takes her by the arm and stops her. An old lady, a shawl about her head, comes slowly down the hill and David and Annie stand still and quiet until she's gone.

"Annie, listen," says David at last, "we must talk."

"Why don't you leave us be?"

"I'm no harm."

"Like a bad penny, you are . . . leave us be."

"Let me talk . . . just for a little while . . . please."

"All right, but not here, not in the street."

"Where, then?"

Annie pulls her coat about her and seems to drift across the road. David follows as she moves towards the bridge then suddenly turns right through a gap in a stretch of hedge, moves down a long, dusty path and through a tunnel of trees. She moves like some ghost as branches and ferns part before her and it gets darker and thicker with foliage. They hop across stone islands that span a little stream, haul themselves up a bank by the trailing roots of trees and eventually walk around the rim of a large natural basin.

The Devil's Dip this is, and dark and strange it is,

too, with a coolness amounting to damp. The village children play here, their imagination sparking among the shapes and sounds, their voices muted and stretched with secret fears. Over on the far side of the dip there's an old hut, almost covered with weed and tilted with decay. The children say the Devil's friend lives in this hut and that sometimes they see him walking slow among the trees, looking for children. They say he has a face at the back of his head as well as at the front but that he keeps the back face covered with a piece of black cloth that hangs from his hat.

Annie moves to where some long, low branches form a cave and sits on a piece of log. David sits beside her feeling strange and nervous, the sweat of the walk cooling quick on his forehead.

"Are your parents still in the chapel?" asks David as he watches ants scaling the boulders of dust by his feet.

"Yes . . . there's a meeting . . . but I won't stay long."

"No."

"It can't go on for ever, you know, you calling on us, we've got our lives to lead."

"Jenny had a life to live, too."

"It's old ground, best forgotten. We're a devout family, David James, and we've been punished a thousand times for what my brother did. You can't punish us any more." David stabs his foot among the ants, creating Armageddon for them.

"I'm not trying to punish," he says. "Believe me."

"Then stay away," says Annie, as cold as the words.

"I try to."

"You keep coming . . . reminding . . . what are you trying to do?"

"I don't know . . . perhaps just to find some help . . . I don't know."

"No one can help any more," says Annie, sitting ungiving and another life away. "You mustn't come any more, not ever, my parents are getting very angry, they've had enough."

"And your brother?"

"He's gone."

"Gone?" David turns in surprise, he hadn't known of this.

"He left over a week ago," says Annie, and her words are heavy, as though speaking of someone dearly loved, but dead. "He just packed his case and left for London. We don't know what's happened."

"The army, perhaps?"

"Perhaps."

"Fancy just leaving," says David, still taking in the news, "just like that."

"Anyway, he's gone."

"I'm sorry . . . really, Annie, I'm sorry."

"Dad doesn't care, Mam cries."

"And you?"

The question finds no chink. "Leave us alone," Annie says, "that's all I ask."

David kneads the palms of his hands into the back of the log as he searches for something to say, something that matters, but nothing comes, nothing that matters. So he just hears himself talking, saying nothing much, about how he hopes he'll find some love, and Annie, too. Hears himself asking why love is so terrible, why it brings only pain.

"Too many questions," says Annie. "We'd best be going if there's no more to say."

"You believe in God, don't you?" David says, sharp. "One of the believers, aren't you? Well, ask Him to send me some love. Ask Him to sweep down from the clouds and bring David James some real laughter before he forgets the sound. You ask Him, and that Mam and Dad of yours, get them to ask Him too, get the whole damn village to go down on its knees . . ."

Annie cuts him short. "Stop feeling sorry for yourself," she says, "it's time you wiped your own nose. Perhaps you'll find some love one day, if you stop running."

"Words, Annie, just words," says David. "Would *you* touch me? Would you?" Annie stays still as though made of wax and David goes on, "Touch me, go on, touch me, touch me."

She doesn't though, she remains unmoving, staring straight ahead through a hole in the leafy cave down towards where the stream slides among the darkening trees and the last of the midges hover above it.

"You see?" says David, moving close to beside her and feeling their thighs touch along their length. Stays like this, unmoving, as the sounds around him go behind curtains and there's only the feel of her leg against his and the scrubbed smell of her and her breasts like small mountains beneath her coat. If only the lights of the world would go out now, now at this second and there would be utter and complete darkness and silence. If only in the thick, black quiet their lips open and distorted on each other, kissing, licking, sucking, whispering, their hands gripping, stroking, scratching vicious to blood, their bodies naked, writhing, jerking in an agony of pain and pleasure and release, he could find the beginnings of an answer.

The world, though, keeps its evening light and Annie sits in simpleness, her hands in her lap, as though suddenly prepared to sit here patiently while all the tomorrows pass and there be an ending to things. Slowly and almost without realising what he is doing David brings his hand across the front of her coat and slowly opens the buttons till the two halves of it fall away and then the hand slides over the surface of her black satin blouse and the fingers open the buttons there too. Then the never still fingers find the strings of her chemise and pull gently at them till they slide through the eyeholes and allow him in.

Under her chemise goes his hand and then contracts softly around the swelling of her breast. Slowly his fingers massage, squeezing, pressing, letting the nipple free between them, rolling it there while her heart beats into the palm of his coaxing hand. He watches her mouth, intent, waits for the lips to part and pull back from the teeth. Waits for her eyes to close in the special

131

drowning and for the first moan to start from the centre of her mind.

Stay closed, though, do her lips and open her eyes and the whole of her is still and dead and quiet. He takes his hand away, out from the warmth where he wishes his tongue could go swimming, and rests the hand on his knee. His urging, sea-anemone hand has brought the breast up from the concealment of her clothing and left it exposed now outside her chemise. He looks at it lying there, white and rounded against its pillow of satin black, and aches for the taste of it. Annie leaves it uncovered, sits in her awful stillness, like a corpse being mauled.

"Please go," she says, and the words come soft and well-mannered from the cold, God-praying lips. David suddenly longs to snatch her by the hair, pull it out through the scalp, throw her to the ground and with his belt beat her and degrade her into the earth. Longs to see her mouth wide and crying among the dust and the ants, to scream with sickness as he rapes her dead, unkissing, God-praying lips. The world is filled with marble people in idiotic isolation. Their cries are unheard, their tears roll unseen down the inside. Could a continuous and biting whip bring blood from the marble? Could a merciless lashing find at last a sort of love and hugging and a warmth of goodnight kiss in childhood's bedroom, while Arabs watch?

"Please go," she says again, unknowing of his thoughts and David rises weary from the log and moves away outside the shelter of the branches.

The dark is gathering quick now, Nature getting ready for the night in long shadows is altering its shape. Had the man with two faces gone walking by at that moment it would not have been surprising or out of place.

When David turns to look at Annie she is easing her breast into its secret darkness and quickly and mechanically fastening the buttons. Together they walk from the Devil's Dip and as they go down the side of the bank.

David remembers the day that he and his father had stumbled down the mountain, separate, and his father crying out "You asked me to tell you, you *asked*."

Across the stream go Annie and David, up the long, dusty path to the hedge that skirts the road and there they stop and look at each other, survivors from some wreck. Lights now shine dimly from the chapel opposite, but even if it's God's house, surely He's not at home, not in that place, not ever.

"Goodbye, Annie," says David.

"Goodbye," she says, and with no more word turns from him and begins the walk up the hill.

"Oh, Annie," he calls after her, and she stops and faces him while he says, "If ever you see your brother, or write to him . . . tell him it doesn't matter . . . in the long run nothing really matters."

She nods, then continues her slow ghost drift homewards as David watches her go, before he turns and walks away across the bridge on the long walk back to the farm.

TWENTY

By the time David finally reaches the farm he is staggering with tiredness and his head aches from thought.
Thought of what he'd done to Annie, and why? For
what reason? He hadn't intended it, heaven knows, it
had just happened, sudden and daft and now regretted.
Thoughts of everything have crowded his mind on the
long walk home, thoughts so thick he hasn't even noticed
the day go out, especially thoughts of Iorweth . . .

Iorweth, the only one untroubled by the deaths, the
only one seemingly happy because of them, happy in a
secret special way that bothers David deep and turns his
mind inside out with terrible suspicions. He turns now
into the yard of the farm, sees a light shining from a
window and heads across the cobbles towards it. Sleep
will be nice now, he looks forward to it, hopes it will
come, a release from thinking.

Then he stops halfway across the yard for he can see
another light, a light coming from the barn and he
moves wondering to the worm-eaten door of it, creaks it
open and goes inside. The light is coming from a storm
lamp standing on an upturned box and as he looks
around David sees the old and rusting implements glowing in it, implements from years ago when the farm had
been a busy place and many men had worked in it.
There's old cart wheels, too, and harnesses, a large sieve
hanging from a meat hook and wearing a veil of cobwebs
and an impotent bucket trying to hide its holes with a

piece of sacking. David turns slow as he hears a little laugh from the top of the hay loft, peers into its shadows, hears a rustling.

"Iorweth?"

"I'm up here."

"What are you doing in the barn at this time of night?"

"Come up the ladder, I want to talk to you."

For a moment David pauses, there is something even stranger than usual about Iorweth's voice, a gleeful madness that warns of trouble, but David does his bidding and climbs the ladder to the top. Iorweth is lying full length on the hay, his head resting in the pillow of his hands, a smile on his face.

"Yes, David," he says, "a little talk. I think it's about time, don't you?"

"Talk about what?"

"Oh, about Annie Rhys, for example," says Iorweth, slow, dropping each word like pebbles in a pond and happy at the ripples.

"How did you know I was going there?" Iorweth draws up his legs and crosses one over the other.

"I found out," he says, "Mam and me found out. We'd been wondering where you'd been running off to . . . wondering we were." David grips tight on the edges of the ladder. Found out? How? Had Mr Rhys visited the farm and complained of David?

"Bit nosey, aren't you?" he says.

"Oh, I'm interested in you, David boy, very interested. Your odd little ways interest me. Now I wonder what made you keep going to the Rhys's?"

"I don't know myself."

"Wonder what draws you there," goes on Iorweth, remorseless, "like a moth to the flame? David the moth, burning his wings and starting to enjoy it."

"Enjoy it?" laughs David. "You're crazy."

"Yes, enjoy it. You're beginning to wallow in pain, enjoy suffering. Jenny loved you, you didn't care. Dad loved you, you didn't care."

135

"Rubbish, man, rubbish."

Iorweth sits up sudden and crawls forward on his knees.

"All you care for," he says, and his voice is vicious now, "is the thing you can't have, but you keep pressing your nose to the shop window, wanting it. Well, Mam's love is for me and for me alone and all your weeping and wailing and punishing yourself at the Rhys's won't change things. You've more than outstayed your welcome, David, boy, much more. There can't be two of us for Mam, it's not possible."

David stares close at the wild face of Iorweth, sees the sickness in the eyes, the slackness in the mouth, smells the drink about him now.

"You're drunk," he says.

"That's right," Iorweth replies, giggling, silly again and getting unsteady to his feet. "That's very right. Look, here it is." From the hay at his feet he pulls a bottle and holds it high above his head. "Dad's brandy. I took it from the cupboard. I've drunk a lot . . . wicked I know, but there it is. I've been lying up here for a long time, drinking and thinking . . . thinking of *you*."

"Thinking what?"

"Thinking you're like grit in my eye and I want you gone."

"And if I don't?"

Iorweth hurls the bottle savagely into the hay behind him. "There's plenty of places you can go," he shouts. "Plenty. You don't have to go to London, there's places here, places in Wales. Go to Fishguard or Anglesey or to the cockle women of Towey . . . go anywhere . . . anywhere."

"Does Mam know you're drunk?" asks David, his voice calm.

"Go anywhere, David. Leave us alone, leave Mam and me alone."

"And if I don't?" says David for the second time.

"And if you don't I'll kill you."

"You'll what?"

"I'll kill you, David, then the settling bees will add another to their score."

"Kill me?"

"You think I won't?"

"I think you're really mad, really mad, Iorweth."

"Empty words," Iorweth shouts back. "Empty words, they mean nothing."

"Well, I'm *staying*."

"I'm warning you."

"This is my home . . . you won't frighten me, boy."

Iorweth staggers towards him like someone in a snow-drift, his finger stabbing out like a dagger. "Jenny died," he shouts, "Dad died . . . you'll die."

David leans sudden across the top of the ladder. "They died because of you, didn't they?" he says.

"That's right," replies Iorweth, the wildness subsiding in him to something colder, more deliberate, something crueller. "They died because of me."

There is a pause now and the wild dog barks in the distance. David seems frozen to the ladder and Iorweth moving away from him to the back of the loft gives a little nervous laugh.

"I knew," says David at last, "I knew."

"Clever old David," says Iorweth, sneery, "shall I tell you about it?"

David nods, but keeps his eyes on Iorweth. Iorweth sits in the hay, picks up the brandy bottle, takes a long drink from it and after giving a cough and spilling a bit across his knee he looks up at David and wipes his hand across his mouth.

"Well," he says, "it was like this." Then he lies back again, cupping his head in his hands and going silent. David moves on the ladder and reaches out with his foot.

"Don't move," shouts Iorweth, sitting up. "If you want me to tell . . . don't come near me."

David moves back on to the ladder. "Go down a rung," says Iorweth.

David does so, and waits again while Iorweth takes

137

another long, slow drink from the bottle. Then he puts the top on it and drops it into the hay. David waits patient, frightened to spoil the moment.

"Well," says the sitting Iorweth, his elbows on his knees, his head between his hands, "this is the way it was. When Jenny did that terrible thing with the Rhys boy I made her feel so . . . day after day I told her that she would . . ." He stops for a moment, then goes on. "She became ill, David, real ill, ill with guilt . . . and I kept at her, never letting her be, not for a moment, never letting her forget what a sinful thing she'd done. Never . . . never . . ."

David's head lowers in the pain of Iorweth's words and Iorweth smiles to see it. "Then one morning," he continues, "she just looked at me . . . looked at me different . . . stopped crying . . . and walked away into the barn. After she'd gone I lay down for a long while watching the wind bending the trees over me . . . then I got up and came here." He stops speaking for a moment in the memory of it, then finishes. "She was hanging from that beam there, that very beam, only she wasn't properly dead, still jumping a bit. So I sat on that tub in the corner . . . and waited . . . and in a while she stopped . . . and later I cut her down."

The story has come simple, as though Iorweth had been merely describing a journey of little importance and David feels a terrible anger starting in the stomach of him.

"And Dad?" David prompts, but Iorweth only laughs and starts to search for his bottle again.

"Tell me," says David, his voice scarce able to keep the lid on his anger.

"*Wait*," shouts Iorweth. "You damn well *wait*." The moment is his and he knows it and he savours it as he savours the drink which this time makes him cough for quite a while. Then he looks up, crafty like a fox, and laughs again to see David staring at him, all interest.

"Tell me, Iorweth," says David quietly.

"Well now . . . Well, now," says Iorweth, measuring

138

the words. "Yes . . . he slipped all right, Dad slipped all right . . ."

"But?"

"But he'd got himself a hold . . . hanging there he was . . . saw me coming through the rain . . ."

"Go on."

"He called out to me, called out for help, said he couldn't hold on much longer . . ." He pauses, looks straight into David's face, watches the story putting pain into the eyes.

"Go on, Iorweth."

"Well, David, boy, I just stood there . . . and he kept on calling . . . couldn't believe I wouldn't bend down and help. Then he stopped calling . . . and I waited till he fell away."

Again the story had been told flat, factual, no feeling. Not on the surface anyway, not where it shows.

David is breathing deep, gripping tight on to the ladder, his knuckles white and the inside of him a volcano but the voice is cold like an iceberg.

"I knew that's how it was," he says at last, "knew that's how it was, I knew."

"So leave us, David, before it's *you*."

"You've said too much, Iorweth," David says, his voice changing, growing harder, and Iorweth smelling the change backs up a bit and watches careful like a snake. "This time you've said too much."

"I know the score," says Iorweth. "You can't hurt me."

"And Mam?" David asks it quiet. Iorweth's eyes dart, the change has thrown him.

"What about her?"

"She can hurt you, can't she? Can't she, Iorweth?"

Iorweth scrambles back closer and says, "Not Mam . . . not ever . . . not ever."

"She hurt you when she struck you."

"She didn't mean it."

"Of course she meant it."

"Shut up."

"Of course she did, of course she did."

"You're lying, you're . . ."

"She broke the cord, man, face facts, face bloody facts."

David comes another rung up the ladder. "She began to see what she'd made of you and you know it, too, don't you? Is that why you're up here on your own? Is that why you're drinking? It's over, isn't it, Iorweth? She talked dreams with you and you made them real, she talked pretend wishes and you made them facts, mad Iorweth made them facts."

"Shut up, now!!"

"But it was only *you* who wanted the things to be facts. Mam just wanted the dreams and wishes, that's all, a fairy story to keep out the cold. She thought she wanted revenge, made herself believe in it but it's not what she wanted at all, not at all, boy, all she wanted was a little love."

"She's *had* love," screams Iorweth. "From *me*, from *me*."

"Oh no, boy, not love, you've never given her love, you don't know *how* to love and now she's realised it herself."

"You're so stupid," snarls Iorweth, like an animal. "So damn stupid you make me sick, you don't know *anything*."

"Neither does Mam, does she? Does she, boy? Doesn't know the half of it."

"Leave me alone, I'm tired of you."

"Indifferent to the deaths of Jenny and Dad? No, more than that, much more than that, *caused* the deaths. What will she say when she hears that, Iorweth? You've said too much."

Iorweth stops as though shot through the heart of him, his eyes widen while inside his head things fall to bits and his voice comes out shocked and pleading.

"Don't tell Mam," he says. "Don't tell her."

"It's over, Iorweth."

"Don't tell her, please."

"Of course I'm going to tell her."

"Please, David, don't tell her."

140

"For God's sake, man, do you think everything you've just said can be forgotten?"

"Please don't tell her."

"It's got to be told and you're coming with me."

"No!" shouts Iorweth, starting to back away, but this time David leans forward sudden and unexpected, grabbing Iorweth by the shirt, pulling him close, holding him tight. Struggles and writhes in the grip does Iorweth, a dog desperate to get out of its collar, twists and pulls and kicks out with his legs. One foot cracks into David's elbow and the other connects with the ladder and sends it sliding along the edge of the loft, leaving David hanging by one hand. The other hand moves quick and seizes Iorweth's ankle, the nails digging into the wool of the sock, pulling Iorweth out over the edge and together they fall in a shower of hay to the barn floor.

Lights burst now in David's head and a dull burning pain from his knee puts the taste of sick in his throat but he scrambles to his feet in time to meet the rushing Iorweth with a wild blow that misses the head of him and lands towards the back of the neck.

Iorweth hurtles away, colliding with one of the cart wheels and falling awkwardly on it, his arms among the spokes. David is on him in a flash now, pulling him from the wheel, twisting his hands into his hair and dragging him face downward across the floor.

"Come on," he screams, hauling Iorweth like a sack of potatoes but Iorweth's hands come up, grab David by the arms tearing the shirt arms to shreds, then the skin of the arms and David lets go. Only for a second, though, a second while Iorweth rises, his breathing terrible and his eyes crazy, then David lashes out with his fist and it cracks into Iorweth's face bringing an instant jet of blood that spurts up into his hairline.

For a moment it seems that Iorweth will fall but he is kept erect by hatred, hatred that brings them both lunging together again, their heads banging, bringing more lights and pain and a thin crescent moon over David's right eye. Locked together in sweat and hate they roll like a crippled spider across the floor, twisting, kicking, punching and crashing into a tilted ladder, breaking its first two rungs and sending it spinning against the far wall. It bounces twice, pirouettes on one leg then slides slow down the wall, bringing with it a collection of tin cans, jam jars filled with rusted nails and finally unhooking the large sieve which breaks free from its prison of cobwebs and clatters off into a corner.

David's hands tear now at Iorweth's face, the blood smearing everywhere and as Iorweth twists and squeals like a stuck pig David hauls him to his feet by his shirt collar and pulls him again toward the door. Iorweth stumbles and falls to his knees, coughs as the blood trickles down the back of his throat but David keeps his hold on the shirt and pulls him to his feet so savage that the shirt buttons fly away like tiddlywinks.

"Come on, come on," David shouts again, gritting his teeth and pulling vicious at the coughing, bloody Iorweth. "Come on."

"Let go of me," Iorweth cries, going on his knees again and then pitching forward, his face staining the hay. No mercy though, not now, not from David who has become a man possessed and who now reaches out cruelly again to heave him upright.

"Get up, Iorweth, get on your feet, *get up*." Iorweth is pulled to his feet but, finding strength from somewhere, he breaks free from David's grip, almost falls backwards over the bucket, but stays upright.

"Leave me alone," he says, "I mean it now, leave me alone." David, though, has no intention of leaving him alone, not now, not when everything is going his way. So he crouches and stalks until he sees that Iorweth has his back against a wooden strut of the loft and then he moves in quick. Again his fingers find and grasp Iorweth's hair and pull him, yelling, forward. Then his arm goes round the head and locks tight against his body, as he begins to half pull, half drag Iorweth toward the door.

"Come on," says David again. "*All* the dreams have got to be spoiled."

"I was *lying*," Iorweth calls, his voice muffled against David's body and his own body bent double and awkward, like someone in the stocks. David tightens his grip and pulls harder.

"Too late for all that," he says, wrestling Iorweth against the frame of the door. "We're going to have some truth now."

"You'll be sorry . . . I warn you . . . you'll be sorry."

"The truth . . . we're going to have the truth."

"You'll be sorry."

"The truth."

David lashes out now with his foot and crashes open the door. Pulls the writhing Iorweth out of the barn and into the yard and the night. Strange now to see them struggling in the darkness, their boots clattering on the cobbles, their hands gripping, exploring, finding holds. Fingers finding eyes and squeezing, elbows turned to battering rams, they fight in an odd silence, something like a dance and the moon lights them for a moment as they fall, turning over and over.

In the living-room Mrs James sits in her rocking chair and stares before her without seeing. She should have been in bed by now, indeed had intended to go, the thought had come to her but not the movement, and so she has stayed, sitting, and let the day die around her without noticing. Pictures in her head click and go, nothing sticks any more, everything is just fragments, time has become confused.

Endless sudden remembrances of her husband Robert, the sight and sound of him, the terrible need disguised as silence, the years of waste hidden in hate. Robert? Was it Robert lying over her in the hotel bedroom while people laughed and sang below? Which hotel? When? Sunshine now, sparkling in thousands of tiny lights on plates and cups and crockery in a long ago kitchen and Mrs James young and singing turns to see someone standing blackened against the

143

sunlight in the doorway. Who? Who is it standing? Who?

The man speaks, looking wretched. "I'm sorry to say this, Mrs James . . . it's about your husband . . . about when he went to Cardiff." The day goes black, no singing now, remembers wiping a plate as the man speaks on in a voice which tears everything, wiping the plate, the plate with the picture of the . . . forgotten. . . . Plate? . . . Which man?

Who is the girl becoming part of the water's brightness as she dances slow? Robert looking at her . . . a dream? Nothing sticks any more, long stretches of blackness and just bits of things . . . Robert and Iorweth and David and Jenny . . . bits of them. Sees her hand on her dress, a hand white and lined, an old hand . . . old already? Already? Old already?

The song she'd been singing in the kitchen before the man had spoken . . . what was it? What was the song? It had been a song she'd sung before as she'd run through crumpled countryside after kissing Robert full on the lips when drizzle had made them shelter by a rock. Remembers running ahead of him, laughing, twirling, spinning and then singing the song. What was the song? About a girl . . . that's it, a girl and her new bonnet, yes, that's right, that's it.

Noise? Fighting? What is it? The door behind her is thrown open violent and David and Iorweth stumble in, bloody and breathing hard, rattling the room with their struggle.

"Tell her," screams David, holding Iorweth by the shirt collar and pushing him forward. "Tell her! ! "

"Tell me what?" asks Mrs James, holding tight on to the arms of her chair and floating in uncertainty. "Tell me what? What's happening?"

"Tell her!" David shouts again, and from the mouth of him there's a trickle of blood which rolls away off his jaw and makes red buttons down his shirt.

"What do you want, David?" asks Iorweth, pulling himself sudden free from David's hold, so that his shirt

144

is tugged over one shoulder. "The truth? Is that what you want? Or what I told *you?*"

David looks across at his mother who has turned away from them both, like a child suddenly bored, and she rocks now to and fro, seeming not to be part of things. He crouches beside her chair and places his hand on the arm of it, stopping its movement.

"Mam, listen," he says, but she silently removes his hand from the chair and starts her rocking again, so David goes on regardless. "Mam . . . Iorweth has just told me everything. He *made* Jenny kill herself by making her feel so evil and unloved that in the end she had to do it for peace and when he'd forced her to do it he just *sat* there, Mam, he just sat there and watched and was glad."

Iorweth bursts out laughing now, roars with laughter and collapses into a chair and Mrs James hearing his laughter smiles herself, not understanding.

"And Dad, too," goes on David, gripping the chair again, "Dad, too, Mam, on Craig Point. Iorweth could have saved him . . . but he didn't . . . he just sat there again . . . sat and watched and didn't care." David sees his mother's expression change from vacancy to puzzlement, feels he is making progress, follows up his advantage. "That's your Iorweth, Mam," he says, close to her ear, "that's your lovely son. He as good as murdered them. You talked of bees and wild tales and he made it happen."

"He's lying, Mam," says Iorweth. "Don't listen."

"No, Mam," says David, still close, "I'm not lying, he told me . . . in the barn. Don't let him deceive you again, Mam, not again." Mrs James sits in stillness for a moment, absorbing what has been said, then, in a strangely formal way she turns to Iorweth and says,

"What is David saying, Iorweth? What is he saying?"

"Lies, Mam, that's all, just lies."

"What did he mean about Robert and Jenny?"

"Just lies, Mam, don't listen to him."

David jumps to his feet. "It's *you* that's lying. Tell Mam what you told me in the barn just now, tell her the *truth*."

"Go to hell, David," says Iorweth, in the chair, and then suddenly feels half choked as David grips him by the shirt collar again and yanks him to his feet.

"Tell her!" shouts David, shaking Iorweth like a rat, "Tell her the truth!"

"Let go of me."

"Tell her the truth."

"All right, David boy," says Iorweth, breaking free and staring fierce into David's eyes. "If you want the truth you can have it, but don't say I didn't warn you."

"What do you mean?"

"I mean Jenny's death had nothing to do with me."

"Tell the truth."

"It is the truth. It wasn't because of me she killed herself . . . it had nothing to do with me . . . nothing. I didn't make her feel guilty or any of that stuff, she felt it enough for herself. Once you left home she was finished, ask Mam, ask her how she used to walk around the farm as though in a dream or something, ask her how we used to hear her crying at night. The only reason she killed herself, David boy, the *only* reason, was because she thought you had gone for ever."

"And what about Dad?" asks David, not believing a word of all this.

"He *was* dead when I got there, he *had* slipped and fallen, perhaps hours before I arrived, I don't know. But do you know what I really think happened with Dad?" Iorweth moves closer to David. "I think it was the same as with Jenny. There was no reason for him to go to the edge of Craig Point, the fencing stops twenty yards away, no need to go further, especially in a storm, hardly able to see for rain."

"So why did he go?"

"I think Dad killed himself, deliberately."

"For God's sake . . ."

"Deliberate, David, deliberate, killed himself deliberate like Jenny, because like Jenny he thought he'd lost the only thing he cared about . . . your love, David boy, your wonderful love."

"Don't listen to him, Mam," screams David now, "don't listen to his lies, he's twisting everything."

"It was you who made him tell the story of the Cardiff girl," Iorweth goes on. "*You made him* and when you'd forced him to tell it you turned from him, didn't you? Didn't you?"

"Yes, but . . ."

"Oh, David, my good, good, David, you didn't care for anyone. I'll be honest with you, David. I didn't care about Jenny and Dad dying either, after all it brought me nearer to Mam, but the difference is that I wasn't responsible for their deaths, like you. I wasn't responsible. So you see, boy, even if you don't like it, the truth is that we're both exactly the same, you and me, both the same, both wanting the same thing. In the barn just now I let you think I was to blame because I was silly with drink and because I thought I could frighten you away. I didn't want to say all this, not at all, I'm not as bad as you comfort yourself by thinking, I just wanted you gone, that's all, just wanted you to go, but you kept ferreting around, couldn't leave things alone, forced me in the end to tell, like Dad, forced me to tell. So, there you are, that's it. Jenny and Dad are gone because of you and that's the truth."

"No, Iorweth . . ."

"That's the truth."

"Mam," David cries out, stretching his arms towards her like a baby wanting to be picked up, but she only stares ahead and calls out, "Oh, sweet God, help me." He moves quickly to her side, takes her hand in his, kisses it, holds it tight enough to break the brittle bones, rubs it against his cheek.

"I'm sorry, Mam, oh I'm sorry."

"Help me."

"I didn't mean for . . . I didn't think . . ."

"Help me."

147

"I only wanted . . . you shouldn't have . . . why didn't? You should have kissed me."

She pulls her hand back sudden as though it's being burnt. "Don't touch me."

"Mam . . . Mam, please . . ."

"Don't talk to me, don't talk, not *ever*."

She moves now, unsteady, towards the door, walking through an invisible swamp, seeking escape, peace. David goes after her, spins her around by the arm so that she almost falls and has to grab the dresser for support.

"I didn't want them to die," he screams, "I didn't want it."

"Too late for sorrys," says Iorweth calmly, now sitting strangely quiet in a chair, "the days have gone."

Leaning on the dresser Mrs James, the face of her white and ill, seems to be speaking to someone not in the room as she asks:

"What have we done, all of us? What have we done?"

Iorweth moves slow from the chair, approaches her cautious, takes her arm gentle, smiles and says "Come on, Mam, I'll help you to bed."

"No, don't touch me," she says, pulling away, and stroking the spot where Iorweth's hand had been. "Don't touch me, either of you . . . do you understand? Either of you. There's nothing but sickness . . . leave me be."

"Don't turn from *me*, Mam," Iorweth says, and his voice is still calm, "we've got to stay together, we've got to or there'll be nothing."

"There's already nothing," she says.

"Mam, listen . . ."

"Nothing, there's nothing. From now on there'll be walls between us, walls for always . . . from now on we'll be separate . . . separate . . . separate . . . the three of us . . . separate."

Iorweth and David stand still like soldiers, on guard in silence, listening to the hall clock tick, feeling the walls already growing around them, watching as Mrs James shuffles to the door in her own strange separateness, opens it and goes out into the darkness of the hall.

"You'll need a lamp," Iorweth calls out, but she closes the door on his words.

They stand for a while just looking at the closed door then David says,

"She blames herself. She blames herself for everything."

"She shouldn't blame herself . . . it was Dad's fault."

"Nobody's fault," says David, "it's all nobody's fault."

"Then why has it happened?"

The answer is locked away in a thousand different things and there's no time now, the time has passed. Things have been done, or not done, things have happened and now there's only blame to hang, watching over everything.

TWENTY-ONE

Iorweth wakes suddenly, his eyes flicking quick in the blackness of the bedroom, his body tense. Slowly bits of the room come at him out of the dark, a patch of ceiling by the window, the water jug, the edge of the wardrobe. He lies wondering what has wakened him—some sound perhaps? But the room is quiet save for the creak of his bed and the countryside outside is still.

Then the window glows as the moon comes from behind dark night clouds and puts a shaft of light across the bedroom, a shaft which spotlights the top half of David's bed. The sheets on the bed change colour with the moon, blue they look, and flat and the pillow is a blue tombstone at the head. Iorweth lies looking at David's bed for a few seconds, watches the moon dying on the sheets, sliding to the floor and going out. Only slowly does the thought come to him that the bed seemed unnatural flat, the pillow empty of head. He listens in the darkness for the sound of David's breathing but there's no sound. He quietly calls out David's name, no answer.

Out of bed now gets Iorweth, fumbles with a box of matches, lights the oil lamp and carries it across to David's bed where its light shows that the bed is empty indeed and folded neat. Iorweth notices now that the wardrobe door is open and when he looks inside he sees that David's things have gone, all trace has gone.

How long ago, wonders Iorweth? An hour? A few minutes? Was it David leaving the room that had woken him? It is only when he moves towards the door that he sees the note propped against the water jug and picking it up he reads the hastily scrawled message.

"You've got your wish at last," it reads. "I've gone. I'm going back to London and I won't be coming back, not ever, I don't suppose, there's nothing to keep me now. Mam's all yours, Iorweth, all yours. David."

Iorweth reads the note over and over, taking in what has happened, wondering why David has left at this time, hours before the train will arrive. He doesn't know that David, his suitcase heavy in his hand, is saying a slow goodbye to everything. To the farm, and the road to the village, and the cemetery, where now he sits by Jenny's grave and his father's grave, saying goodbye to them without talking, as the moon lights him like a lighthouse.

Now David rises and leaving the graveyard to its awful peace he starts the long walk to the village where he will stand and say farewell to Annie's house and to the Devil's Dip. Maybe tonight in the Dip the moon will show a glimpse of the two-faced man as he scurries among the trees on Devil's business.

He walks on down the road, changing the suitcase from hand to hand, stopping sometimes, remembers the times he has ridden this road in Daniel's cart—poor Daniel . . . Goodbye Daniel. Walks on, every step a goodbye, a goodbye to everything and everyone—the fields, the hedges, the trees, the stones, the murmurings of Nature and the very smell of Wales that fills him now like his own blood and becomes more part of him than ever. Walks on as Goblins chatter unseen around him, walks on, cutting himself to pieces with every stride, saying goodbye to himself as well.

Holding the lamp ahead of him, Iorweth moves out of his bedroom, along a bit of landing, illuminating for a moment another picture of Arabs and camels, down two stairs and then to the dark brown door of his mother's bedroom. He opens the door and enters the room which has the sickly sweet smell of age and sickness. Mrs James, her face turned yellow in the oil light lies with her eyes wide open, staring at the ceiling as though she sees pictures there. Iorweth, who has expected her to be fast asleep, approaches the bed cautious, kneels by it, and touches her arm with his free hand.

"Mam," he says quietly, unsure. "Mam."

Her face turns slowly towards him till their eyes meet, but the eyes of Mrs James don't alter, their surface stays dead. Her head has all the pictures it wants, it has no need of eyes to add to them.

"All over," she says, her lips hardly moving. "All over."

"David's gone."

"Down the stairs," says Mrs James, seeing it all somewhere behind Iorweth's head, remembering the sounds. "Down the stairs . . . creeping . . . out into the yard . . . away."

"You heard him go?"

"All over."

Her head turns away again and looks up at the ceiling and Iorweth, realising that he doesn't exist for her, rises and goes out, leaving his mother and the room to darkness.

Goes back now to his own room, puts the lamp on the stand beside the water jug and soap dish. Sits on his bed looking at the shadow of himself on the opposite wall wishing there was something to be said or done, anything. Sits as time goes by, his thoughts roaming unformed, his shadow thinning, growing smaller, the lamp spluttering, and then, as fears bring on shivering, he rolls into his bed, pulling the clothes over him like a cave.

TWENTY-TWO

Although the day is bright with early sun, the farmhouse seems to make its own shadow and stand lifeless in it. Inside, a lot of the furniture has gone, leaving a patch of freshness where it has stood and the stuff that remains stays only because it is too big or finished.

Like the beds in the boys' bedroom that are now side by side in the centre of the room, while their mattresses tied with string bow to each other in the corner. Spared at last from the pressure of bodies and the bite of springs but bearing coiled rust marks like tattoos. The rose-covered wallpaper is as thin as corpses skin and the colour in the roses seems to blow away before the eyes.

In Mrs James' bedroom the bed remains where it has always been. The bedclothes, though, have gone, and the pictures and vases and little boxes and bits of life and by the door the dresser shows its empty paper-lined drawers. In the open wardrobe one of Mr James' old suits hang limp and alone on a hanger, the turn-up on the left leg hanging down, showing a bracelet of dust.

The uncarpeted stairs, odd and naked, seem wider and unfamiliar, while above them the varnished hand-rail worn smooth and dull, holds a thin line of sunlight along its length. The kitchen, too, seems sudden large in its emptiness and on these walls too are startled patches where things have been. Under the sink a wooden box is filled with chipped and broken crockery and beside it an old frying pan stands on its head, showing across its fat the paw marks of a mouse.

In the living-room Mrs James, as lost as the house itself, sits in a chair her mother had loved but from which now the inside is spilling like white and furry blood. Behind her the piano stands waiting for whatever will be, too old and sick to bother with, it bares its yellow teeth, smiling, smiling, inviting music, just once, however out of tune.

Strangely dressed in a three-piece suit Iorweth sits on a suitcase, staring out of the window. Listens for a moment to the steady tick of the hall clock then realises that it can't be so for the clock, like so much else, has gone. Some things though, he thinks as he sits there, have left their mark like the clock—Jenny playing in the orchard and David and his Dad laughing happy into each others' faces as they stand in the hall, shaking snow from themselves like dogs from the sea. These things, and many more, will always be around, little ghosts going on, whatever happens, whoever comes.

Mam, though, has gone for ever, although she sits now in the wounded chair, her fingers plucking unconsciously at its injury. This is not the Mam who stroked his hair and kissed his lips and talked of love and promises. That Mam has gone, leaving behind a stranger who sits and stares in a time and Wales of her own. A stranger who sleeps more and more, seemingly uncaring as other strangers come and take away her furniture and life and talk of sales and deal with things.

> Therefore as the fire devoureth the stubble
> And the flame consumeth the chaff
> So their root shall be as rottenness
> And their blossom shall go up as dust.

Staring through the window Iorweth looks out across the yard and now sees Daniel bring his horse and cart in through the gate and up towards the house.

"Come on, Mam," says Iorweth, getting up from the suitcase, "Daniel's here, it's time to go." He helps her to her feet and marvels at the thinness of her, the lightness, like air.

Daniel's cart is clattering outside by the window as Iorweth picks up the cases and opens the door for his mother who, hobbling painfully on her stick, steps outside without once looking back. She stands for a second in the frame of the door, her face without expression, her movements without purpose, the bright early sun almost showing the skull beneath the skin.

"Morning, Mrs James," calls out Daniel cheerily, "morning, Iorweth." He eases himself down from the cart and comes over, all smiles, to Mrs James. "The rest of your stuff got to the station all right, no bother," he says.

Mrs James, who only seems to find movement when people speak to her, turns her head at the sound of his voice and their eyes meet and Daniel sees a long-ago pain there.

"Come on, now," he says, gentle. "Let me help you, give me your arm."

"No," she says, her voice a harsh whisper as she pulls back from him, "no." Iorweth has loaded the suitcase and now sits on the side of the cart watching as his mother walks stumbling and unhelped towards him. She refuses his hand, too, as she climbs aboard, slipping, gasping, then sitting strangely erect, filled with ghosts and Daniel, who has watched her awful progress to the cart, fits his smile back into place and moves towards the horse. He climbs up with some effort, it gets harder all the time these days, and picks up the reins.

"It's going to be strange," says Mrs James, her voice suddenly clear and alert.

"What's that?" asks Daniel.

"Going to be strange," she says again, "not living here."

"Going to be strange not having you here after all this time," replies Daniel. "Still you'll be fine where you're going—and don't worry about the old farm, I'll look after it till the new folks come. Are we all set then?"

Behind them the wild dog begins its loud yapping in the shelter of the orchard.

"Lovely day, anyway," goes on Daniel. "Crisp and bright and the promise of heat." He jerks the reins and the large wheels creak forward taking them across the cobbles and towards the road. Suddenly Mrs James calls out, and her voice just keeps down the panic that shows through the words.

"I don't know where I'm going," she cries, "I don't know where I'm going . . . and I don't know why."

"Friends," explains Daniel hastily, "you're going to friends, Mrs James, they'll look after you."

The panic in her subsides and she sits back calmer, deader. "Yes," she says quietly, "yes, that's right."

"No friends, Mam," says Iorweth, sudden, putting the words in like a knife, "no friends at all . . . just me."

"Lovely day," says Daniel as they turn into the road, but there's no reply from Mrs James who second by second is pulling back inside herself as Iorweth watches.

"Talk to me, Mam," says Iorweth, his words urgent, scalpel probing, "you've got to talk to me . . . Mam . . . you've got to talk to me."

Mrs James, though, sits in her other-world stillness, huddled and removed in her large grey coat and the fur collar of it putting a nest around her throat, the scenery breaking in pieces on her eyes and the bits falling on her wandering mind.

Daniel, sitting upright, is glad to lose himself in driving, making great play with the reins and happy that the horse's hooves are putting a frame of sound around the silence at the back of him. Wishes to God now that years ago he'd never got talking to a cattle man called Price who had just returned from Cardiff and who'd told him of what he'd seen there. Wishes to God, does Daniel sadly, that, troubled by what he'd heard from Price, he'd not visited Mrs James and told her of her husband and the girl in Cardiff. Remembers for the thousandth time the way his words killed her even as she stood there in the sunlit kitchen, wiping a plate over and over, long after it was bone dry and shining.

Too late now for words or love, too late for a long, long time, so Daniel sits stiff in his cart, narrows his old and secret eyes against the blue of the sky where puffs of white clouds are stuck like cotton wool on a Christmas shop window.

Iorweth pulls away from his mother in final acceptance of things as they are, as they'll always be. Lets his head loll forward on to his chest, his hands hang between his knees. There'll be no getting better for Mam, no long walks in the streets of town, him in his red jersey, her in her hat.

Mrs James begins to sing in a low, far-away voice, a song Iorweth has never heard before. She sings as though the words were coming from somewhere else, a song about a girl and a bonnet, then she stops sudden and goes silent again.

"Certainly is a nice day, anyway," says Daniel, who wishes the horse could eat the miles in a second and there could be an end to everything, for ever. "Very nice, indeed," he says, answering himself, "thank God for small mercies."

Down the country road they go, the horse striking steady and the cart wheels wobbling out of true with the unaccustomed speed. On through the miles until they're clattering across the old stone bridge in the village where the Rhyses live. As they go over the bridge, ahead of a dog that yaps its anger at their wheels, Mr and Mrs Rhys are standing in their garden of flowers. Unexpectedly Mr Rhys puts his arm around his wife's shoulders and gives a squeeze of comfort and their eyes meet, though who knows what they see there, for although the Lord may have forgiven them their sins, they themselves can not.

From the bedroom Annie watches them moving among the flowers, sees her father's hand slip away from her mother's shoulders, watches and wonders what the days will bring, the years will bring. Wonders if she'll ever see her brother again or if his bedroom door will ever be unlocked. Hours later she suddenly beats at that door with her hands, beats at it savagely till the bruises come and the sound of the frenzied battering echoes through the house.

*   *   *

157

The train begins a slow hard climb and with Wales falling away on each side it snorts and puffs its way upwards, a descendant of the dragon.

In the last but one carriage Iorweth and Mrs James face each other without words, and Iorweth, his dream destroyed, feels he's taking a corpse to burial. Nothing but deadness between them as they sway in a slow, stiff dance to the rhythm of the train. The miles go by and the face of the country changes to a more gentle look and Iorweth, listening to the creak of the carriage, and watching the sunlight making holes in his mother's lap sees that although her head is low as though she is sleeping her lips are moving. He leans in closer and hears that she is saying "Robert" over and over, saying it sad. So he turns his gaze from the slowly moving lips and looks from the window, seeing nothing now, only hearing the endless "Robert" falling on to her breast.

The train goes on and on, pointless, a knife through the butter miles, pointless, leaving Wales behind in its smoke, clanging through the gentle green, but nothing is really changed. Iorweth's face is still pressed to the glass, looking without seeing, pointless, and Mrs James, sleeping again, sways like an old doll and everything is pointless, now and always, pointless.

Who sees the terrible dream in Mrs James' head? Who feels the pain in Iorweth's stillness? Who knows what Daniel feels as he sits at home now, unable to eat for sadness and blaming himself for everything. Poor Daniel, who will soon be in the cemetery, lying close to Jenny and her Dad, everything over at last, the dead the only tidy things.

Therefore is the Anger of the Lord kindled against
    his people
And He hath stretched forth His hand against them
And hath smitten them and the hills did tremble
And their carcasses were torn in the middle of the
    street.

TWENTY-THREE

Anonymous in his uniform, David moves among the jostling khaki of the troopship. Above him seagulls scream, dive and level out over the quay where crowds of people run about, seeking, searching among the acres of khaki for a familiar and loved face. Others wave handkerchiefs or flags, smiling and laughing by turn and holding each other in a trembling uncertainty. Others just stand as though turned to stone, neither moving nor speaking or indeed being part of the day. It is as though the face they seek without success on the troopship's deck is already dead and belonging to another time. Slightly wild laughter ripples through the crowd as an elderly soldier bearing a great drum on his chest wobbles towards a waiting band like an old fat duck.

David leans on the ship's rail, hearing other Welsh voices around him, and singing on a lower deck, but he stays apart from everything, waiting for the siren and the casting away of chains. Then it comes, the jar of the siren reverberating in every piece of wood and glass and metal, and the great deep drumming of soldiers' boots as they all rush now to the rail and wave. Wave like a vast field of wheat as the military band below them manages at last to sort itself out and strike up its oompah music.

The soldiers are running everywhere, shouting, colliding, shoving, laughing, some fall, others lose their caps, which float down into the docks to the accompaniment of fresh cheers. Others, their faces alarmed as their ribs are pressed further and further against the rail, try desperate to push away without success, and all around there's the swelling sound of whistles, hooters, cheering and music as though sound and movement itself will hide the crying and the troubled thoughts.

David, though, just leans against an iron pillar away from the rail, letting it all go on without him, although the sound pours in his ears and explodes in his head. On and on it goes, an over-loud, over-long goodbye to things and people and the security of knowing. David, who has said his own goodbyes long before, moves away from the pillar, climbs to the upper deck and watches the bow of the ship tear the sea which boils and settles back to the rhythm of waves and hears the sound on the quay wane and break like an old, tired clock.

To the watching soldiers it seems the land is pulled away from them and they watch the figures of those they love and may not see again grow smaller until they cannot be separated from the quay, and the quay from the docks, and the docks from the land which is now far away and stretched thin in the distance.

David breathes in the salt wind and feels release in the distance each second brings. There's no Jenny in this wind, Dad in this sea, ghosts among the following gulls, Mam, Wales, memories, in this cold, clear place. He laughs, and the laugh is carried into the wake as he feels for the first time something near to peace. He watches the sea widen, stretch, deepen, building water walls between the now strangely silent and wondering ship and the slowly disappearing, silent, twinkling lights of home.